LADDER IN THE WATER

AND OTHER STORIES

FEROZ FAISAL DAWSON

PARTRIDGE
A Penguin Random House Company

Design by
Bright Lights at Midnight

To order additional copies of this book, contact
Toll Free 800 101 2657 (Singapore)
Toll Free 1 800 81 7340 (Malaysia)
orders.singapore@partridgepublishing.com

www.partridgepublishing.com/singapore

table of contents

appreciation

••••

I thank every friend who lent me money when I was broke. A writer's life would be impossible without begging for and borrowing money that will never be repaid. I thank Faridah Merican, my mother, who still believes in me after all this time. I thank Yvonne Teoh and Lynn Yap who typed all my early drafts for free, and the KLPAC girls who collated the stories. This is a book of fiction, but I thank my friends for giving me ideas and subjects. I thank Christine Spisak who typed and organized the later drafts – and spoke her mind. And my editor, Thor Kah Hoong, who fought with me and forced me to deal with reality. I like working with people who fight with me. And I have fought with most people on this list.

at the county library

● ● ● ●

I was sitting cross-legged in the library with the French section on my left, the Roman section in front of me and the Japanese section on the top two shelves two sections to my right when a black kid walked into my home with the intention of re-shelving four books I had returned two days ago. I recognized them. 'Late Chrysanthemum' - a book of Japanese short stories from the thirties onwards; two books of Japanese poems, one hundred poems each; one volume also had its hundred poems printed in Japanese calligraphy. The last was a book of French writing with English translations. The same old gang; Voltaire, Balzac, Maupassant.

Naturally I made to move because I was sitting where he had to shelve them. He stuck every single book, side by side, in the English section next to Agatha Christie. French and Japanese in the English section. I would never have found these books again had I not been sitting on the floor in that spot in front of the Romans with the French on my left and the Japanese above. And I wasn't done with them yet.

I was sober. Or rather I did not have beer breath on account of drinking a 24-oz can of Steel Reserve in the men's room. I drink one can a day because my wife doesn't want beer in the fridge. I don't blame her. If it were up to me I would have 15,938 cans of beer in the fridge; so I drink my one beer a day in the men's room of the library. Keeps me from thinking about it all day. And I drink that one beer in the last stall on the right as you enter the men's. I chose that stall because it is larger and is the only one that has a hook on the door and a railing on the side because it is for handicapped people. I've never seen a wheel chair in there so don't judge me dear reader. Yes, once, I saw a man on a walker and I demurred.

I did not have beer breath because there was a pair of shoes in the stall two doors down. There was something going on because when I went in his shoes were pointing out and when I left ten minutes later his shoes were pointing in.

I spend a lot of time in the men's room looking at the floor because I only drink and burp when there is no one else in there. Sometimes I have to wait twenty minutes. I sit quietly. When the door slams and the man in the next stall has gone, I roar my burps like a lion. Guys used to do that when they were young, when girlfriends were scarce and marriage an impossibility. Always drink on an empty gut. I cannot get drunk on one can but I can get a buzz and like the television ad says driving with a buzz is driving drunk so you could say I drive around the library drunk; actually I sit down a lot, shut my mouth, and avoid children.

I didn't drink on account of the pair of shoes in the third stall. And because I did not have beer breath I could go to the proper authorities when I saw what that black kid with the glasses did when he re-shelved the books I returned two days ago in the British section. That's what I told her, a lady with red hair and red glasses, "He put them back in the British section,"

"He put them back in the wrong place,"

"Yeah, yes,"

She nodded very slowly, like a cobra. "Is he back there right now?"

"Yeah, yes, black kid with glasses."

She went after him so fast I thought she was going to fire him and I tried to stop her. "I don't want to get him fired or anything," She said, no, no, she was just going to talk to his supervisor. That's the thing about people in America, they move even before you've finished talking.

The pair of shoes doesn't know it but because of him justice was done today. I went back to the handicapped stall in the men's room. I opened the Steel Reserve, drank it and walked home. Alcohol is not allowed on library premises. You could lose your library card.

The black kid with glasses is still working at the county library. Ordinarily I wouldn't squeal or rat someone out, but it is a question of books after all.

a drop
of silver

● ● ● ●

It was near the end of 1990. Charles and I got drunk, and we decided to take a drive. The government had decided to hold a general election for the grateful, happy and prosperous citizens of Malaysia.

It was also Visit Malaysia Year. A huge success, so they say. Millions of customers, I mean visitors, crowded our shores, spending many millions of dollars on accommodation, transportation and the developing of millions of rolls of film. All this commotion provided millions of jobs for Malaysians (who were previously doing unimportant things) in the lucrative, fast expanding service sector. Malaysians, after all, are such delightfully polite people and like nothing better than to serve people.

There were billboards everywhere, courtesy of the government, reminding us to act our natural, courteous selves when dealing with visitors. Everybody was always smiling on these billboards and the policemen (or were they the tourist police — the idiot cousins of inbred policemen?) were always showing the way to thankful, blissful blonde foreigners. The policemen were always smiling too, and the men, in particular, always had very fine moustaches.

There was also a profusion of election banners and posters bearing political party symbols and photographs of candidates strung from tree to lamp-post to traffic-lights, pasted on walls and bus-stops and poles stuck into the ground.

At first, the agreement was that I would drive and Charles would jump out and cut down whatever campaign material belonging to the ruling party he could find. I got impatient seeing him do all the hard work, and joined him at what he was doing, going my own manic way. We would achieve more destruction in half the time.

Redressing the balance, that was why we did it. Of course, we didn't expect it to make any difference but we had a good excuse (especially after four big bottles of stout) and it was once in four or five years, an Olympian interval, and we were bored.

Don't judge us unkindly. How could anybody match the machinery and labour the government had at its disposal? A mammoth machine of incumbency was up against all these little Davids, these Robin Hoods, these tiny desperate wretched opposition parties. That was what we thought of the situation, especially after four big bottles of stout. So you can't say we were vicious, cowardly hoodlums resorting to childish inane acts and worse, trying to justify it with the excuse of supporting the underdog. Life is not much fun when the favourites win all the time. The slightest chance of an upset and the nerves are all tingling, alive.

After all, we grew up on Enid Blyton, with her Secret Seven and her Famous Five (when I think of how far I've fallen since St. Mallory's; oh, the shame, the shame!), also not forgetting important primers such as Beano, Dandy, Tiger, Battle, Roy of the Rovers, Shoot, etc. The point of this has to do with the R.A.F. outnumbered at the Battle of Britain; going out to bat with a broken arm and scoring

70; the underdog triumphing at Wimbledon. "We like underdogs," say Charles and I.

The axe was mine, the parang Charles'. We set out to cut down and destroy as many Barisan Nasional posters, banners, flags as we could. The rain had stopped, you could hear loud, noisy frogs booming, moaning, in between the hissing of the tyres of cars on the wet road. It was between 2 and 3 a.m., there were very few cars out. The last thing Charles and I wanted was for somebody to see us chopping down banners and posters, and stopping and beating the shit out of us. I could imagine a bunch of tough, bigger guys coming out of their car and I would have to run. What about the Police? What if a police car were to stop in front of us, while we were trashing around? Shit, they have guns, semi-automatic weapons, if they saw us with our instruments and thought we were both Indians, they'd probably blow us away for sport. As it is I'm half-Indian, so that makes us one-and-a-half little Indian boys.

Of course, all these hypothetical situations did not impress themselves upon Charles as he was bounding and leaping from lamp-post to lamp-post, tree to tree and across the road and back again. With me, of course, it was a different matter, not because I was more sober, more inclined to be realistic. It was just plain cowardice.

We decided to concentrate on one particular road. The road was straight, long (so long it had two names), started at the roundabout next to Charles' house and ended at the roundabout near Guru's house. Here, people seem to get around town by landmarks. Not for us the tiresome chore of remembering road names and numbers, as they are so many. At Charles' roundabout it is a billboard put up by Rothmans. Thus, "I went from Toshiba to Rothmans and after that, stopped by F&N. Later, I beat my wife in front of Guinness," and so on.   The name of this particular road from the Rothmans roundabout, intersecting Sections 19, 17, and 12 to the University Hospital traffic lights, which is then sawn off by the Federal Highway bursting through underneath it, is Jalan University.

Jalan Gasing begins across the flyover over the Federal Highway past churches, a couple of chicken rice shops, a pub and a 7-Eleven, past the massive gold and white Buddhist temple and boys' and girls' schools, separate of course, Indian restaurants (one of them Rajoo's where my grandfather went every day at 6 a.m. for years until he got too sick and infirm and couldn't drive and nobody would take him there, especially at 6 a.m), to the turning to Bukit Gasing.

Like I said, we started out with me driving and Charles jumping out and hacking down the posters and banners hung on raffia string and thin, green plastic rope. There were posters stuck on squares of plywood with a short wooden spike nailed to the back; these were thrust into the ground, which was wet that night, having rained earlier. These were kicked down and stepped on. The first half of our pointless, but, we hoped, symbolic destruction, was achieved quickly, quietly, smoothly. I kept the engine running while Charles did all the hard work, or had all the fun, tick one answer whichever applicable. I said, "Charles, hurry up, c'mon let's go. Charles!" He would turn around with a grin, parang held aloft, while he half-strutted, half-ran, with chest puffed out. "Wait, hey, you missed that one." He'd turn around, leap, swish, turn, big grin.

I don't remember many cars on the road that night. Four years earlier, election night, Charles' mother wouldn't let him out of the house. Sunny's mother let him go only with the greatest of reluctance. Both mothers never forgot the tumultuous, harrowing carnage and destruction which followed the election of 1969, 17 years earlier, the only time racial riots became loud and dangerous enough to forever undermine the heretofore laissez-faire attitude of the government.

The time had come to examine and monitor the insidious, treacherous activities of people. Henceforth, citizens and politicians would not be allowed to participate in mass gatherings of discontent. These would have to be held behind closed doors, for a limited number of people; no more public marches. The risk was too great, the opportunities for development and growth and advancement too precious to mismanage.

Who's to say they were wrong in doing what they did? Iisn't an opinion in hindsight not worth the paper it's written on? Stability, safety, that's all they cared about, not justice, fair-play or truth. God forbid truth. Developing countries can hardly be expected to cope with the frank, vulgar, naked face of societal reality. And they wonder why no respect is given, why the lack of enthusiasm, why the lethargy.

Now, where the hell was I? Ah, yes, reality, truth and lies, what charming, civil, topics. As long as it's printed in the papers, that's truth enough for most; sanctified statements repeated on all three television channels, repeated with a straight face, slight smile, to be taken for the truth, nothing else but; not to be made fun of under any circumstances (nobody ever did), nor to be discussed at length. Which is why we seldom heard the final word on a particular subject or indeed, any opinions with regards to matters that were in the public eye, but which disappeared with all the secrets and chains of guilt attached, sinking with the ship, and its captains out of sight and therefore, out of mind.

Never mind, as long as we have stability, peace, foreign investment. We're in the process of catching up, why nitpick over the details? It was a fait accompli, there was no question that the government would be returned to power, the only question being, the size of the majority.

After three bottles of stout, we felt it was our duty to redress the balance. Cut down the ruling party's banners and posters and leave the opposition paraphernalia standing, then maybe those going to work the next morning might chance to look at the dewy, wet grass with its blue and white posters lying face down in the damp unattractive grass of the dividers, roundabouts and sidewalks of the well-behaved, quiet, peaceful suburb.

It wouldn't have made any difference. It just would have provided those early morning cogs or captains of industry a few seconds of early morning cerebral activity. Eyebrows lifted, eyes opened wider, ears assailed by the news of football matches on the car radio; wondering why anybody bothered to knock down those posters and cut down those banners. Maybe the wind did it, some may have thought, but they would not of thought of that too much, their own lives having to be sorted out first.

Who the hell were we kidding? We didn't do it for anyone. We did it so that we would have another shiny, diffused memory to talk about in our later years, when no one would believe us, when we were left with only our thoughts and deeds to keep us company. We could say and think, with a ripple of pride, "Yes, we were hard core. We did this, we did that, we did such and such." We'd repeat these stories to anyone who would care to listen, until the inflections and pauses would become automatic, identical, the deeds would gradually become mightier, more astounding, and then that too would become automatic, identical, and our memories will then blur the distinction between what did and what did not happen.

My grandfather used to drive his tiny, matte pale green Morris with my cousin and me to the barbershop every time he thought we needed a haircut; which was often, seeing as when we were little our hair did not grow so much as sprout. Rahman's barbershop was in the middle of a row of shop-houses on a crest of the road that we were on that night.

Rahman's had four chairs, with a long mirror covering the entire length of the wall facing the chairs. The wall opposite in this narrow shop with a high ceiling had a narrower, though just as lengthy, mirror which was set about head high for adults as they sat in chairs. The mirror was slanted slightly downwards towards the backs of the four chairs making it possible for customers to see the back of their heads. The front of the shop had two rectangles of glass, the smaller piece, part of the door, had an outline in blue of a man's head in profile, the hairstyle exhibited consisting of short hair at the back, medium sideburns and a voluminous amount of hair in front, combed back yet puffed out giving a somewhat hip Elvis without the ducktail look. The larger pane of glass had the word "Rahman" in large black letters and 'Kedai Gunting' underneath it. No barbershop would be complete without the cylindrical, rotating, candy-striped frontispiece found at the top of the door.

Four chairs he had, but Rahman was the only barber, so there was a lot of waiting. This though, I never minded, probably the only time in my life I never minded waiting for others, for in the first two drawers of the counter on which the long mirror rested, precious as gold, constant as tides, were old tattered, battered copies of Beano, Dandy, Shoot, Tiger; devoured and studied. There were two metal-framed chairs, around which were wrapped thin, multi-coloured strips of plastic, some of them broken, hanging, sticking out defiantly and rigid at all angles, vibrating slightly as weight is shifted. There we would sit, waiting, I head down, scarcely breathing, devouring those crackpot, incredible stories. I'd look up, and Papatok (grandfather) would be sitting, large, relaxed, blissfully silent, loving the quiet, the slightest smile on his lips.

So we were there, at the roundabout. If we went left, we would be on the road called 16/1, the stoically named main road of Section 16. My grandfather lived there, with my grandmother, in the house of his eldest daughter and son-in-law. On the right at 3 o'clock was the road which had two schools, primary and secondary, where I had 11 years of education.

So we're at the roundabout, the Sultan Abdul Samad boys school (secondary) on my right. Charles jumps out before the car stops. I jump out. This is my school we're talking about here, our school; I've got things to uphold. What things? Daring, showing off, standing ground, stepping forward, speaking out, nods, winks, sign language, deeds, memories, the past to uphold. We hear the swish of cars on the wet road in the distance. We snap our heads at the sound, look, hear, hearts beating faster and louder, nothing, we continue, he cutting, I cleaving. Nothing is said. We jump in, doors are slammed, engine chokes, then dies, the starter strains, I press the accelerator down halfway, a roar, we continue up the road; sweat, silence, then a chuckle.

Our school used to have the biggest field in PJ. S.A.S. was made up of two levels; buildings, classes, the canteen, the hall, the staffroom, labs, were all on the sunken, lower level, whereas the huge field was set higher, 15 feet above. The football and hockey fields were separate, the grass track around them 400 metres; at one end a pavement, concrete basketball court, at another, a narrow cricket net containing one strip, cement being the surface on which batsman faced fast bowlers. Two tiers of grassy slope surrounded this haven of activity. The football field never had any grass in the middle of the pitch or in front of both goals, where a semi-circle of black, grey earth was always in evidence. Lush grass proliferated along the sidelines, green, hopeful, inviting. Our skins were burnt black and shiny doing laps around the hockey field at 11 in the morning. We were nothing if not fit. I wish I was now. There was only near silence when we trained. Apart from the master's voice there would only be puffing and panting and the squeak of rubber soles on grass, rushing blood and pounding hearts obliterating all sounds. Sweating in silence, we never complained. We may have been tired, but we recovered quickly. Youth, the death of which is more unbearable than that of death itself, so said Mishima. Sartre said that if you don't get it on by the time you're 25, you're fucked for life. Now, there are buildings on my school field. The track is gone and so is the basketball court and they're going to forget the hockey pitch, keeping only the football field. If, in cricket, you hit the ball into the compound of the new buildings, you get two runs, if you hit the building themselves you get four and what was a short square-leg boundary is now reduced to farcical, nonsensical dimensions, but who gives a shit anyway.

Slash, down went the posters, crunch, the plywood squares were split.

"If you want to read the truth, read fiction," some woman said. Damn straight. Never mind soap operas, musicals, and science fiction to describe how a solitary leaf falls to the ground, that's fiction, that's literature, that's the truth. OK, OK, too dogmatic, why so dogmatic? Passion obliterates reason, as so it should.

"Charles, do you want to stop?" That's what I thought, not what I said.

"Mak, got some more left, ah?" That's what he said as he dived under the dashboard, to jerk back up with a big bottle of warm stout, held high in his right hand at the bottlecap edge, reflexive, on to the aluminium clasp, which is what the door of my car clicks on to as the door is shut, holds on to, despite the rattling of screws and things on account of the rock-hard, non-absorbent suspension; the aluminium ring the door shuts on is the perfect bottle opener. Sssstt. Bottle opened, it is tilted to Charles' mouth, one gulp, two, three, four gulps, then it drops to his knees, followed by a sibilant "Aahhh!" which gives way to a low burp and then he shoots the bottle under my nose.

It starts to rain again. I welcome it, thinking it must be good because now it would be harder for people to see us in the rain. Charles disagreed. "It would be easier to see us because in the headlights, the rain will look bright and the light that is reflected from the rain will make it easier to see the surrounding area."

I used to walk, sometimes run, to school from my house 300 metres away. And still I was late, reason being I would leave with just five minutes to spare from the start of school. Sometimes the prefects would be late getting to the gate, and I would get away with my tardiness.

Charles, a prefect, used to chase me and Sunny back to my house (giving the impression of someone in authority chasing truants) where we would hang out. This running was good cover in case the police, usually in the form of two men puttering about on a 100cc bike, known colloquially as a 'kap chai', happened to stop their ominous crawling and turned back to ask questions. Charles was the man to talk to, word perfect in Malay and English and fluent in Cantonese.

There were two levels to my garden; at the back of the house the garden was about five feet lower than that which encompassed the front of the house. Cricket was played on the front garden. Along one end ran a dark, cool, mossy brick wall in front of which the batsman would stand. There was no room for a wicket-keeper, unless someone bowled spin, but we were young and nobody would bowl spin; everyone bowled as fast as he could. Even the regular spinner bowled fast. Bowlers could take six or seven steps which would take them into the gravel driveway separating the two parts of the garden.

Charles, Pandian, Chee Aun, Douglas, David, Alex, Kai Chong, a lot of us played there; ebullient, exuberant, tireless. The road in front of my house was Jalan University. A grey wire fence separated the garden from traffic. The way we played, a shot to square leg was the most rewarding in that the ball could travel the furthest distance; it would roll over the five-foot drop, continue through to the back garden where the fence would stop it from hitting the neighbour's roof. Behind the batsman, all leg glances invariably bounced off the wall and on the off side all nicks were caught from behind. If you pulled the ball to mid-wicket, the car in the driveway and the front door of the house with its attendant narrow windows on either side would be in grave danger. If you hit finer than mid-wicket and in front of square-leg you were liable to injure the small, high windows of the master bedroom, bathroom and store room. An on-drive would be most judicious as the ball traveled all the way to the fence on the other side of the garden. An off-drive was ok, but if you hit it too high and over the fence, you would hit and maim people sitting at the bus-stop which was practically never empty, it being a busy road. Apropos off and cover drives, everyone would look with mouths opened in speechlessness as eyes traced the arc of the road-bound ball, and wonder whether there would be any cars coming on to the path of the ball. When that happened everyone would be running, bat taken and stumps forgotten, over the five-foot drop that separated the front garden from the back garden, and all would jump off, roll and would crouch low, straining, to hear any sounds of doom. All would be stifling their giggling except perhaps the offending batsman who would look worried.

We were at the last roundabout; the one in front of Guru's house. It was packed with posters and banners, it was not possible to knock down and flatten all of them. Charles was trying. We were at the end of the road, the end of the night. After this, there was no need to go on. I looked at Charles. He was trashing wildly, quickly. I thought of running over and helping him. I didn't.

There was not even a single car in sight. I, feeling constricted, could not get into a frenzy. I snapped the last meagre poster. "Charles, let's go, man, come on."

"No wait, Mak." Around him the posters cracked, split and flew.

"Come on, Charles." I crossed the road, running towards the car. I had seen two yellow beams of light. I stopped running, walked instead, hiding my axe. Charles stood up, parang in hand. The car stopped for a while, then drove off.

Charles wouldn't stop. This was stretching it too far, pushing luck and denying ratiocination. We had been let off, why not get the flying fuck out? He bounded across the road. Fear had all but smothered me and I was in my car looking left and right. Slash, slash, slash, Charles was winding up, he was going to finish, then the car door slammed, he was in the car, we were safe. Huge sigh of relief, then a chuckle, broad smiles, satisfaction, a job brilliantly done.

I started the engine. A small van shot in front of us, parked diagonally. We were blocked. I reversed instantly; we didn't scream or yelp, only gasped and forswore breathing. "Not to worry," I thought, just reverse and bugger off. Bang! We hit something. I threw my head around to look. Another van had parked behind us.

I pulled my steering wheel hard right and cut past the front van and on to the road. (Thank God for small Japanese cars.) Charles had begun biting his fingernails. I pressed the accelerator full to the floor. This was where more worrying began because it was still a question of two vans chasing the slowest car in town. And those vans were quick even with three or four bulky passengers. The top speed of my car was only 140km/h. Much cause for concern. I didn't shit in my pants, however, and should be commended thus. Charles was quiet, biting his fingernails, while I was chattering in a high pitched voice, repeating over and over, "Oh shit, Charles, fuck man, oh shit, Charles, die man, we're fucked man. Are they coming?"

The road was long and straight, and the massive old trees in the middle and on both sides obstructed the white light street lamps, leaving it in near darkness.

I couldn't see headlights in my rear-view mirror and as I relaxed, I almost crashed into the roundabout in front of Assunta Hospital (which would have been a tragic, coincidence seeing as I had emerged from the very same institution to be added to the world some twenty years before).

Was I in love with her? Of course not. I hardly knew her. All I did was love the way her eyes saw everything, said everything. There was a particular look that I caused and that I will never forget and forgive myself for. We were in Guru's kitchen, as usual in the depths of another stupid, useless, rhetorical argument (nothing like a cheap bottle of rum to draw company and conversation within which one's noblest ideals and deepest secrets inevitably reveal themselves), when after she said something, I gave her a look full of contempt, derision and disgust, more than was intended, but I was so disappointed with her, and when she saw me she said, "Why are you looking at me like that?" Her eyes looked at me crushed, puzzled and betrayed. I felt so ashamed.

I wanted to apologise and say no, I didn't mean it, but I just lowered my head and said nothing, telling myself never again will I look at another that I cared for like that. The way she looked when she sighed, pouting, determined, angry, when she was bored. Restlessness entwined with world-weary wisdom, sometimes sounding so naïve, but she was beautiful. And she laughed, often, so often that it was a tired, lazy laugh, which showed her white even teeth, white under her violently red perfect top lip, the ends of which were curved upwards, with her full, gorgeous, sinful lower lip.

There is a line in Bob Rafelson's "King of Marvin Gardens" where Ellen Burstyn says that false eyelashes are made from minks. "I've been walking around for twenty years with little minks on my eyes." Fiona's eyelashes were long and full, and shielded and shaped her grey green brown eyes, limpid and large, direct and always questioning. One night I looked at her for a long time, she smiling languidly, not flinching, and I said, "Your eyes are green and grey and brown." She smiled and she said to me, "Sometimes they turn blue."

The first time I saw those eyes they were red and heavy with crying. In that split second, I was free. I thought, "She's pretty."

Then I glanced at Mike, who was sitting, stricken, paralysed. It was when I saw Mike's face, plowed, streaked, scarred with tears, that I knew it was real.

Charles was dead.

Guru was speechless, and I was shaking. Guru told me of it over the telephone, "Serious-lah, I'm serious. He passed away this morning. Died on the spot. Jalan Tuanku Abdul Rahman. He didn't suffer. He ..."

He was driving. He clipped a divider, bounced off — into a pillar. On the spot. Neck. 2.45 a.m. Yes, yes, yes, details. Everyone wants to know the details, all the lifeless, dense, pedantic details, questions, the same ones, the only ones.

"Was he drunk?"

"Who was the passenger with him?"

"French, you say?"

"He was working here, or on holiday?"

"Really ah? How long had he been here?"

"That's terrible luck. It's all fated. His colleague sleeping on the back seat, not a scratch. So young. If only these young people wouldn't drink and drive This is the outcome lah." Sighs, pronounced and often, vacant gazes.

What a relief and pure, sad joy it is to be able to lean on a pillar of religion. Sing the songs loud and clear, monotonous, supposedly soothing, caring, understanding, accompanying his haloed and backlit flight to his Creator.

They had a picture of the car wreck next morning in the paper. The number plate was there for all to see. The bookies no doubt stopped taking money for that 4-digit number that day. Charles' number came out 3rd prize. Bookies lost money probably, but none of us bought the number, we were too stunned and distraught. Charles, the gambler, would not have approved, but he wouldn't have been surprised.

He wouldn't have been surprised, too, that we were late for his burial. The funeral we made to ok, to exchange cries and sobs. The church was in the city and the burial was in another town near the coast. We lost our way. We followed the wrong car.

In the church the pastor or father or reverend whined away, advising, admonishing, telling us about our friend, Charles. "Amen" was said, amen for this and amen for that, and still again, suffocating. Amen, whatever works, a crescendo, a strangled wail, a stuttering sob, an involuntary gasp, heads bowed, tears falling, respect for the dead. Respect for half an hour, then on to home and dinner. "Tch, tch, what a shame, what a pity."

The graves around Charles' were orange mounds of earth, with little, dark wooden crosses upon which were written names in white. They were fresh graves, only recently left by heavy footsteps and forgotten after the one visit that was accorded it, presided over by an official of religion and attended by many. There were many such graves and as they were close together and since there were many people at Charles' funeral, people were walking over and stepping on many graves in the rain that day.

Candles were lit and solemnly, reverently, placed on the grave. I remember Charles' father looking about for a lighter. Wong rapped me on the shoulder and thrust out his lighter, urging me to pass it on to Charles' father. I hesitated and an impatient Wong did the deed himself. I was enfolded by time-stopping, painless, empty inertia, from which I couldn't kick free, wallowing in my weakness, dumb and dazed with rapid bursts of memory, with hypnotic gazing at details seeking relevance and answers, trying to recall happiness, remembering only strange, ugly events; above all, not accepting.

Charles' was the first dead face I'd ever seen.

Alex was the first to know but he never cracked, even as he was revealing the news to us, phone call by phone call, face to face. It only hit him at the wake that we had for Charles at Ting Lam's house. We went there after the funeral.

Who was there? Guru of Norwich, England, Mike Choong of Brisbane, Australia, Wong of Toronto, Canada, Sunny Yap, who never went abroad for studies (through no fault of his own, but that's another story), Kamal, somewhere in Switzerland, Alex Heng of Australia, Ting Lam of course, whose house it was, and yours truly from Penn State.

Guru, a lovely guy, though inclined to be loud at times, was informing us about how great a guy Charles was — "He was ...," "He even ...," "He also ...,"

I was not about to partake. My throat was raw and my eyes felt like they had searing sand in them, and I wished Guru would shut up, even though I knew he was doing the right thing. It was a wake after all, and this was what was supposed to happen, talk about the dead and bring back good memories, let him know how much he will be missed. Alex was crying. "I managed to keep it in for two days, for two whole days, you know, I never, I didn't ..."

"And then he ..." A constricting feeling. I couldn't say, "Goddammit Guru, shut up please!" All I could manage was a look that was supposed to communicate, please, enough. He looked at me, grinned and continued at the top of his voice. He was drunk and vocal and deaf, unlike the drunk and silent, where perception becomes acute, thoughts are focused, skin and nerve ends tuned into the mental climate and physical reality, where the smallest gesture can bring inexpressible joy to your heart or tears to your eyes, where you see through fakes in seconds. Thus even though Guru was drunk, he should have known better, should have been more aware. I mean, I had to sit next to Alex while he was crying buckets and telling me his life story.

Then Kelvin (Orange County) came in through the door with Yvonne (London). They had been on holiday in Thailand and had missed the funeral, missed everything. He said, "I heard about Charles. Is it true, ah?" And then he was choking, gasping and crying.

I was trying to talk to Kelvin, to say anything, everything. Everything sounded horribly wrong, totally idiotic. "Kelvin, hey, don't cry lah, it's ok man, it's all alright, if you start crying again, then I'm going to start again. Oi, you ok? Stop crying, ok? It's alright, man. You see, now Sunny is crying, and if Sunny is crying, then I'm ..."

Alex was bent over crying. Ting Lam was rolling cigarettes and Wong was drifting in and out of the kitchen and living room, always restless. Pete and Fiona were trying to console Alex, but they were nor successful and soon Fiona was crying along with Alex.

In the midst of this cacophony of misery, Kelvin suddenly produced two bottles, duty free, of Jack Daniels. Faces wracked with tears suddenly afforded meagre, trembling smiles. Grief gradually subsided to occasional sniffling. Someone bellowed, "Ah, why never say earlier?" Heartfelt laughter reverberated around the room. Hands rubbed eyes, deep breaths were gratefully taken and sighs were released to signal the approach of some relief.

Some of us thought of not drinking. "Where can? No way, must drink, must drink to Charlie boy. I don't care, can drink, cannot drink, too bad, we're drinking to Charlie," exclaimed Kelvin who slipped into his customary role of MC-cum-bartender-cum-organiser of parties and other such things.

All were herded together to make a tight, close circle. Ting Lam and Wong, who never drank or hardly did, gulped in fear and anticipation, no way out this time. A shot glass was procured, the biggest shot glass I'd ever seen. Sunny almost fainted when he saw it. "Oi, where can man? Gila ah? Not so big lah Kelvin, gifchan."

Kelvin thundered, "This is for Charlie."

"The great Charlie," interjected Guru.

"Ya, the great Charlie, and since you make so much noise, you can kena the first shot." Thus Guru was temporarily quieted.

"Aargg," said Sunny, after he swallowed his shot. All of us were looking apprehensively in his direction as Sunny went through his pre-vomiting convolutions; he was trying hard to control it, to keep it in.

"I think we forget about the shot glass and drink from the bottle," said Kelvin.

"To Charlie boy" became the battle cry.

Everybody grimaced and shuddered, we were not used to it. All the Chinese turned immediately red, and stayed that way.

"Wa laau," said Kamal, as he took his shot. "Wah, strong ah," Alex said as he breathed in sharplym and grinned a sad smile. Mike took his shot and bared his teeth before his jaw set again, and he too nodded and sighed. Pete grimaced and I grimaced and Ting Lam grimaced and Guru grimaced (and started shouting again, soon after) and then Fiona. She didn't grimace, she just drank the Jack Daniels and looked at me with her large, dewy, moist blue, green, brown, grey eyes, and smiled. Did I fall in love with her then? Of course not, don't be silly; it was only after the third or fourth round that I did. She's so pretty and can drink shots, I thought.

So we sat and talked, talked about Kelvin's trip to Thailand, talked about Pete and Fiona's trip thus far, talked about whom we heard it from and when and how, about the service and the funeral and about Shireen, Charles' girlfriend, and how everything was going great for Charles. We drank and talked and smoked and tried to keep it in, tried to hold on. We agreed that no one was allowed to go back, not in our condition. I was glad I didn't have to go home to be alone. "To Charlie boy" was the battle cry.

After we almost hit the roundabout in front of Assunta Hospital, we didn't speak, we were terrified. Charles looked back again and again and finally said there was no one chasing us. I couldn't relax, mumbling, "Oh god, oh god, my number plate. They must have seen the number plate. We're fucked for sure, man."

"For heaven's sake, relax, Mak. Even if they've seen your number plate, you can't do a damn thing about it anyway. I mean, think about it, what are you going to do, huh? Drive to Penang, ah?"

"That's not a bad idea, Charles. Penang is too far, la, but we could drive to Ipoh, to your friend's place."

"Don't be daft, Mak. If they've got your number plate, you can't escape anyway, they'll know where you live. Running away won't help and besides, I wouldn't go away, so you'll have to go alone, and you wouldn't go alone because you'd probably lose your way or something."

"My number plate? They know where I live? This is it, no more crazy stunts, this is just too crazy. I swear this is the last time I'll ever think of doing this. Crazy, cutting down the government's banners, suicide, man, never again, no way."

"Ah, shut up. Thank your lucky stars that we managed to cabut. In this car. Think about it. If your car couldn't start or if you couldn't cut out of there … there were two vans, five or six people each, we would have been hanged, man."

"Lynched."

"Shit, yeah. Tomorrow morning they'd see this car by the side of the road, both doors open, and we'd be missing, nowhere to be found."

"Yeah, after they'd finish beating the shit out of us, which wouldn't be too long, since I'd probably pass out or something, they'd throw us to the police."

"Exactly, who'd then wake us up and continue whacking us. They have things that don't leave marks on your body."

"We'd be in deep shit, I mean, it's beat or death first, talk, if any, later. They don't give a shit who you are. Thank God we got out of there. I never saw them coming. Did you?"

"No."

"I hit the back fucker, man."

"We should take a look to see if you need to go to a workshop."

"Actually, it was your fault, you bastard."

"Me? My fault?"

"Ya lah! You were taking ages at the roundabout. You didn't have to cut down every single little fucking poster. Just destroy some of it, people'll get the idea. You don't have to take down everything. I told you, Charles, let's go, let's fuck off, but you didn't …"

"I was having fun."

"You were hopping all over the place, jump here, jump there. I finished early. I was looking at the cars. There were a couple that passed by slowly, you know?"

"Really, ah?"

"Yah, man, I was telling you, Charles, get the fuck out, let's go, but you were hopping here, there."

"Sorry, lah, Mak, it was intense, I got carried away."

"Well, fuck it, lah, close call. I was really scared y'know?"

"Well, you're always scared. You're the biggest bloody coward I ever jammed with."

"Anyway, as getaway driver I fucking did my job, asshole, and don't you ever forget it."

"Huh, I'm surprised you didn't shit in your pants. Did you?"

"Of course not. Come on, man, I wasn't that scared."

"Yeah, right, tell me about it."

"Yeah, well, lucky we didn't get caught, because it would've been all your fault."

"Up yours, Mak."

"Up yours, Charles. Lucky for you I'm such a brilliant driver."

"Yeah, right, a blind horse with only three legs could outrun this thing."

Epilogue

The Barisan Nasional polled nearly three million or 52 per cent of the votes cast to win a two-thirds majority in Parliament in the eighth general election. The voters returned the Barisan Nasional in 127 of the 180 parliamentary constituencies to give it a fresh mandate to lead the country for another five years.

The onslaught by the Opposition, which saw the Barisan Nasional losing Sabah and Kelantan, reduced the popular votes it received from 57.28 per cent in the last general election.

In the elections for the 11 State Assemblies in Peninsular Malaysia the Barisan Nasional won 253 seats out of 352 contested. It previously controlled 298 seats.

The Opposition obtained 2.4 million votes or 42 per cent of the popular vote against 39.54 per cent in 1986. The Opposition, which carried out an aggressive campaign urging people to vote for a change, won 53 parliamentary and 98 State seats — an additional 11 seats in Parliament and 36 in the State Assemblies. Petaling Jaya, Selangor, remained a DAP stronghold.

I have in my possession, a few photographs of Charles and a couple of postcards, one of which he sent from New York, the other from London. The one from New York is a black and white photograph of John Lennon wearing sunglasses and a t-shirt that says New York City and the one from London has an aerial shot of the Tower of London. This is what he wrote me from London.

Dear Mamak, Apek, Sepet, Ah Seng,

Greetings from very, very boring London. I've been here barely a week and am already bored to death. Not only that, but my balls are freezing as well. Every day is fucking cold. Everything costs a fortune. I joined a protest (candlelight) outside the Chinese embassy on the last day of my exams. Am going to join the demonstration outside the South African embassy.

Charles

fill in the blanks

••••

A Japanese student falls through the air. She is high on paint-thinner. She reasons that death is less terrifying and infinitely easier when one is high. "I'll show them."

A sniper sets his sights on a Muslim boy. The sniper is 19, the Muslim, 13. "I must do this; I made a vow; I must be a man," The Muslim boy is unaware, unafraid; he is seeking revenge. Blood and rubble, dead dogs and live wires. His eyes see, but do not blink, he wants only to hear, so does not pay heed to the smell. His older brother and uncle were murdered; so he picks his way through the grey and white street, in the sights of a gun held by a 19-year-old, heart pounding, vibrantly alive, thinking only of revenge.

A rock twirls, silently spinning through the air. Another Muslim, another country. The rock falls short of the black boots and plastic shields. It splinters, creating a white dust cloud on hitting the ground. The Muslim bends down and picks up a stone. Brown paranoid eyes look at him from under a helmet. Those eyes will remember him. Next time, those eyes will shoot him.

"I hope they spell my name right," said the young man as the explosives are strapped around his chest. "They will, we'll call them and make sure," said the old man.
    The journalist takes the call. "This is the IRA. We are

responsible." The journalist takes a call. "This is the Hizbollah. We are not responsible."

The coffin is inching forward, swaying slightly, gently. The singing is deafening as the black men continue to dance. Some have big grins, some have shut eyes, all are clapping. They dance and dance and dance. The eyes under the light brown eyebrows smile. She has long hair and a toothy smile. The top button of her tight red blouse is undone, showing a little of her 19-year-old cleavage. She has small, high breasts. "No, no," she says, "I don't have a boyfriend; I have no time; I just dance and dance and dance." She will be performing tonight, come and see, she has a great ass.

"I will be on the 13th floor in ten minutes, come and see." The TV crew with the woman reporter who has gaunt cheeks and large dark eyes rush to the building. They make it in time. Glass shatters and a man in flames falls through the air. A protest has been heard. The cameraman follows the flaming arc, zooms in smoothly and expertly, keeping death in the centre of the frame. "What a shot! Get you a jug of beer for that," says the fat, pale man at the TV station.

There is a thin, tall man with hunched shoulders, head tilted sideways. He has the look of a tied-up dog that has been beaten many times. He is always walking, walking fast. He has been walking fast with his head tilted, carrying a solitary bunched-up plastic bag, with that look in his eyes, for more than 10 years. Children are afraid when they see him, but he never looks at them. I remember him from when I was in secondary school. His clothes are the same, only browner, darker, melded to his body, which is as dark as his clothes, the difference being his skin glistens and shines. He is Chinese, I think. He has a moustache, and a forehead always contracted in thought. His arms hang straight down, close to the body. One of them would flap quickly and rigidly, never stopping, while he kept on walking at a great pace.

A postman smiles to himself as he sits in the post office. He has been passed over for promotion. A woman has been given the job instead. He smiles to himself. He is a veteran of war. The air-conditioning has broken down and the heat suffocates. He has made up his mind. He would try to kill her first, but if, as luck would have it, she's not around, well, he would just have to make do with the others. It would be better to shoot the supervisors first. For three years, he has been working with them on his back, remorselessly recording his every mistake. Before he shot them, he would give them a few seconds, just so he could see the astonishment, the time-stopping fear in their eyes, and then he would blow their heads off. Then he would turn the gun on himself. "They'll know my fucking name, then. They'll never fucking forget it."

Save the Whales
Save the Trees
Save the Baby Seals
Save the Children
Save the Rivers
Save the Tigers
Save the Elephants
Save the Dolphins
Save the Penguins
Save the Africans
Save the Muslims
Save the Indians
Save the Ozone Layer
Save the Earth
Save Tomorrow

It was a large pile. I wasn't sure if it would burn or not but the sun shone white, though the grass was a little damp. I held the flaming match at a corner of the Lifestyle section of the New Straits Times. I couldn't see the flame in the daylight, but soon invisible flames gave way to smoke. I stood back to watch. The road with its grass verges and old trees began quivering and wobbling, undulating excitedly, playfully, in the searing sun.

The thin, tall man with hunched shoulders, tilted head and solitary plastic bag, walked into view, barefoot, walking fast. For the first time in 10 years, I saw him stop. He turned and faced me, but remained silent as always. In the heat-waves above the flames, he looked like he was dancing.

I fancied he was smiling, too.

no one has claimed responsibility

●●●●

My, my, hey, hey, I almost saw a riot today.

Mother told me to go to the market, the wet market, the one in Section 14, to buy some fish for buka puasa. She was sitting cross-legged on the floor in the kitchen with a white Persian cat, Ezana Sutra Snowy, in her lap, cutting onions, garlic, and vegetables. The radio was loud.

"Make sure you buy from the Chinese lady only, I don't want you to buy from any other stall."

"Yes, mother."

"If she's not there, her sister will be there; they are the only ones that can be trusted."

"Yes, Yang Mulia. If they're closed?"

"If they're closed, buy from another stall, but they won't be, it's still early."

"Yes, Yang Berhormat."

"Don't forget ikan kurau, two pieces, no, one, no, two lah, if we don't finish, we can keep for later."

"Yes, Yang Berbahagia."

"You knew her son, didn't you? You went to school together. What's his name?"

"Kok Keong, Tan Sri"

"Whatever happened to him?"

"Last time I saw him, he'd just come back from Australia, he was in pre-u, what they call matriculating. I asked him how it was, he said the Australians called him Ching-Chong."

"Really? That's nice." My mother's hearing isn't very good, but her eyes are razor-sharp; she spent her formative years under Japanese rule.

"Take the umbrella with you in case it rains."

"Yes, Yang amat berhormat."

"If they don't have kurau, buy senangin, buy terubok also can, but it's got too many bones, pari also can, but buy senangin first, if they don't have kurau. And don't forget to buy rempah from the Indian man for the chicken curry."

I turned left at the gate and headed towards the mosque at the end of the road. It was a 10-minute walk, and a further five from there to the market.

I hated walking around with an umbrella; it always made me feel a little cowardly. Mine had thick, alternating black and white loops. The sky was a roof of pale grey, I knew it wasn't going to rain; it was still early. I comforted myself with the thought of my mother's chicken curry. I hoped she would put enough salt in it. She was always worried about salt. My mother put so much effort into her cooking, that she could barely enjoy eating it herself.

As I got near to the market, I happened upon a group of irate students.

"Hey, brother, where are you going?" asked one of them, he was shorter than the rest and the frames for his glasses were more expensive looking.

"I'm going to the market to buy fish."

"You can eat anytime brother, join us, come with us, we're going to a gathering."

"A gathering of what?"

"A gathering of brothers, like yourself, like us."

"I don't have any brothers. I only have a mother and she's very fierce."

"Why do you speak like that, little brother? Why the negative energy?"

"I might have inherited it. I didn't mean to be rude. What do you do at your gatherings?"

"We chant slogans, and wave our hands." "Very forcefully," said another.

"Join us brother, in support of our just great cause."

"Is it 'just great' or 'just and great'… your cause I mean. I mean, I don't get you, could you please elaborate?"

"Are you mocking us?"

"I don't have to; you're all sporting goatees."

"You have one too."

"Yeah, but I don't wear it to 'score points.' I'm just too lazy to shave."

"Do you love your country?"

"Yes, especially during badminton tournaments and World Cup qualifiers."

"Arrgggg! Get him, brothers."

The group of irate students made as if to attack. I sprang back, opened my black and white umbrella and pointed it at them. Seeing the umbrella, they turned toward their leader for guidance. That gave me the opportunity to spin my umbrella at a fast speed creating a spiral effect that attracted, fascinated, stunned and hypnotized them. There they stood with slack mouths and wide eyes.

"Yo, irate students, listen," I said, whilst still rotating my umbrella. "Repeat after me, and memorize for life … a little knowledge is a dangerous thing."

"A little knowledge is a dangerous thing," they replied in unison.

"If you play the game your shorts will get muddy."

"If you play the game your shorts will get muddy." again in unison they replied to my words.

"If you leave your house open, you'll have more fun, but some of your things might get stolen."

"If you leave your house open, you'll have more fun, but some of your things might get stolen," they tonelessly repeated.

"Anti-establishment plus power equals a new proprietor, but with the same old dirty shophouse and same old dirty kitchen."

"Anti-establishment plus power equals a new proprietor, but with the same old dirty shophouse and same old dirty kitchen," they mimicked without a second thought.

"Corruption is relative to the size of your country, the lack of ambition and respect for ingenuity. A coalition equals compromise equals more corruption equals no work done. A young country is a naïve country. Naiveté is an euphemism for gross stupidity and ignorance." They repeated every word.

"Tactics are everything in politics, and religion is the dirtiest tactic of all. John Wayne is dead, Steve McQueen is dead. Be kind to all animals, cats in particular, especially Siamese cats." The group echoed me with feeling.

"I will leave you now. You will remain hypnotized for a further 30 seconds, after which you will wake up, remembering nothing of this except that which you have memorized. You will experience feelings of loneliness and emptiness which will manifest itself in an act of violence and destruction. You will want to set something on fire. Might I suggest that trashcan over there, it is full of paper and plastic, it will make for a nice blaze. Once all of your frustrations are out of your system, you will return to your normal chipper selves. You will proceed to your gathering where you will share with your erstwhile brothers the news of your trash-burning exploits. Remember, be kind to animals, and long live Mokhtar Dahari."

As I advanced I happened upon a couple of irate motorists. They were standing in the middle of the road, their car doors open, gesturing and bending down to look at the minor damage. They were circling each other uttering threats.

"You bang my car, not I bang you. Who's gonna pay lah?"

"This one must make police report."

"Why you wanna do that lah? We settle it here enough, I wanna settle it here."

"You tell me how much you wanna settle."

"How I know? Your car kena bang what, not my car, if my car 100 bucks kaotim already."

"One hundred bucks? My friend, 100 bucks my mechanic will laugh at you. At least 400 my friend. This is metallic paint, my friend."

"Four hundred? No way man, this type of scratch also you want 400. We take your car go my mechanic now."

"Go where?"

"Go my mechanic, close by, you follow."

"Eh, friend, you wanna me to follow you go to your mechanic, your mechanic is who? Who the fuck is your mechanic? Why should I go there? My mechanic I know 12 fucking years already. Might as well you follow me than I follow you. You bang my car from the back, you must pay, you think what."

"Who ask you to stop? There's no car coming from the other side, suddenly you stop. Why you stop? Still orange light can go. You stopping for gohost ah?"

"Why you follow so close? Who ask you to follow so close? If I want to stop, I stop ah, if I see ghost, I see ghost ah. You bang me from the back you pay, you think what! Police also no fuck you, your license no need to say … gantung, man, gantung!"

"People want to settle, you still not satisfied ah? People want to settle, what you want some more?"

"Chee sin ah, tiew nya seng!"

"Tiew nya ma."

"Nya ma ke chow hai!"

"Nya ma ke chow chi bek!"

"Ma chi bai!"

"Nya ma ke fu lat!"

I thought about using my umbrella, but it wasn't a case of self-defense, so I moved on amidst a symphony of horns.

The sky was a solid bank of grey. I carried on to the market, the wet market, the one in Section 14. I hated the smell of the market, like esophagus and liver, raw and warm. I preferred to come alone so I could get what I needed and leave. If I were with mother she'd go to the live chicken section just to have a look. I dislike following women round and round, especially when only they know where they are going.

"Auntie, ikan kurau two pieces please."

"Kembong want or not? Today got a lot. I give you cheap. Two katis ok? Take lah." She knew we had lots of cats. "You take one kati ok? Your mother where? Never come ah. You take one kati lah ok?"

"Chicken curry," I said to the Indian man.

The spices were wrapped in banana leaf and then in newspaper. My errand was complete. Worse than the smell was the slime. I was hemmed in between wives, aunts, grandmothers and servants. The women moved so slow, always holding up traffic, haggling over size and freshness, bargaining over twenty cents, poking everyone with their slimy fish heads and wet bushy veggies.

As I walked out into the tepid white light I found myself in the middle of a peaceful swarm, the gathering the young men had told me about. There was a stage at the far end of the street and the street was closed to traffic. On the stage was a little man behind a microphone. I thought I'd listen for a while. The fish were in no danger.

He was dressed in a white robe and serban; a thin, small man standing behind the microphones, five CCD cameras pointed at him. He wore a thin smile and his tiny eyes were watery.

"Brothers," he began, "I share your anger, I join in your disgust. Believe me, what you are feeling, I feel a thousand times more. We, the party, we feel your hunger, we can only try to massage your pain, we know what it's like to starve to death. Starving from lack of food, starving from the lack of justice. We are not like those western worshipping liberal heathens, academics and bureaucrats with their fancy MBAs and doctorates from Harvard, Yale, Cambridge, Oxford and Penn State. This country has been taken away from the people, our people, stolen by the government and we want to give this country back to the people."

The crowd cheered.

"We are trying to stem the tide, to stop the tidal wave of western liberal values which teaches our children to be disrespectful to their elders, to question authority, to dismiss tradition and to have the temerity to ask for and demand equality. These are not our values. Without hierarchy there is anarchy, without respect there is chaos, without belief there is corruption, without fear of God there is vice and degradation.

"Corruption is a disease which our Party shall destroy. All leaders and members of Parliament will be forced to declare their assets. All government, state and federal, contracts will henceforth be awarded in an open and transparent manner. All public works in progress must submit status reports on time with no excuses and exceptions. The days of exemption are over. The age of closing one eye is over. I am sure you will all agree with me that it is about time.

"All pre-election kenduris and open houses will have a budgetary ceiling subject to approval. All government houses will be searched for jewelry, phones will be tapped. We, the Party leadership, shall ensure that corruption, cronyism and collusion will become only a disgusting, appalling and smelly memory of our nation's Sodom and Gomorrah."

There was much whistling and stamping of feet with sustained applause.

"We will protect our children and take care of our families. We must afford them safe shelter, sound advice. And enough to eat. Once we have fulfilled our earthly obligations and responsibilities, we must turn our faces to God to receive guidance and to learn humility.

"All our free time must be spent on introspection, meditation, prayer and sublimation. It is a constant battle to keep ourselves from being engulfed by alien forces that lay siege on our morals through incessant displays of depravity, lasciviousness, ungodliness and perversity.

"Our battle is never won. Our fights are never over, not here on this godforsaken earth, anyway. Eternal victory eternal can only be secured at the heavenly gates."

The crowd murmured their assent.

"We are fair and just to everyone; to everybody we are peaceful and tolerant. We wish to spread the message of unity, but unity can only happen with a total and absolute understanding and the unconditional acceptance of our message. It can only exist under our umbrella of salvation, our tent of truth.

"So how dare they say that we are against unity? That we are in favour of segregation and separation? Absolute nonsense! Only our beliefs can unite all the races. When there is man and woman, we can't expect the man to bear children, to elaborate, only a woman can get pregnant. Only those who believe as we do can get to heaven.

"Thus it was written. To deny it is akin to denying that the sun rises in the east and sets in the west. And I make no apologies for it, nor will I ever do so. It is for them to see the light. And if they wish to live in the dark, so be it, but the day of judgment shall separate the ignorant from the just, pious and holy.

"The Press has painted a terrible one-sided picture of us. They have branded us fundamentalists, extremists, radicals, fanatics. Nothing could be further from the truth. We are fair and just to everybody.

"Friends, brothers and sisters, together, as one, let us go back to the past, to our glorious past and dig out something real and true, something shiny and bright, something we have no doubt of. As it was in the dry, dusty desert, so shall it be in the humid tropics. We shall show the lighted path and we don't care who, what or why we offend.

"Our code, system and rule of law is liberal, generous and flexible; it does not discriminate at all, men and women are treated equally, for example, sports for men and women are not encouraged, especially if it involves wearing shorts and congregating with infidels.

"The use of the term 'infidel' in regular informal speech is to be discouraged. The word 'infidel' should be replaced with 'unholy,' singular, or 'the unholies', plural, or 'not quite so holy' for close friends. For soul-mates who will doubtless burn in hell for eternity, you can substitute 'anthrax.' For contracts, permits, applications, deeds, wills, reports or any legal and binding document, the full and proper term is 'not yet like us through no fault of their own, the silly buggers.' Anything that does not have our seal of approval or nod of approbation will be labeled 'demonic' for serious transgressions, and against the teachings of God Himself for misdemeanours.

"The punishment for such crimes could range from death in a public place to the loss of constitutional privileges and rights. Your citizenship could be withdrawn after a fair trial or you might be removed to an island. I will elaborate on crime and punishment later in my sermon.

"They who dare to call themselves the government, they say many things. They speak of a trickle down economy, but it trickles only to their honey pots, and their honey bees driving Mercedes Benzes, which is why we refuse to ride in and drive those magnificent vehicles that are used to ferry corrupt and shameless government officials in their journeys of greed and self-gratification. When we win the

General Election the party leadership shall ride in Protons. I will avail myself of the LRT. It is peaceful, silent and swift, so I hear. The interstate buses nowadays are not too bad, huge tinted windows, air-conditioning, Bollywood movies, chicken rice, nasi lemak, mee goreng, pillows, blankets, coffee, tea and water free, just as good as an airplane. Even intra-city buses are comfortable and trains are a pleasurable way to travel too, especially if you get a bunk and a sink. We shall ignore the airport limousine service, there are no words to describe that catastrophe.

"That is why, brothers, sisters and friends; why women should not campaign, why they should not run for party posts and public office. It is too vulgar to subject them to such indignities. We respect women and that is why we don't allow them to run for office. An election campaign is no place for the mother of children. It is too too ruthless, too pungent and too upsetting. Men must fight their wars and women must fight theirs; which is, until further notice, guiding their begotten children towards Heaven.

"It is the working woman who is a catalyst for the breakdown of the family; that is a fact. An absence of maternal and spiritual nourishment leads children to a life of drugs, alcohol and general dissipation which leads to a disrespect for authority and society's norms and mores. The breakdown of the family is the first step to the breakdown of society.

"That does not mean a woman cannot become the head of government, that she cannot become Prime Minister. Of course she can, but only if she is married to me."

The crowd erupted and there was whistling and stamping of feet.

"Let us assure you, brothers and sisters, that the first thing we will do, the first action we will take when we assume office, the first policy to be implemented that will set the stage for our fair and just administration will be to force women to wear what we want them to.

"We can't do much about the private sector, but in the civil service all female servants, will be, without exception, required to wear the uniform of our faith, the banner of our belief, the symbol of cleanliness, holiness and piety - the headgear! Our country shall become the headgear nation and we shall be proud of it and be known for it throughout the world.

"If any woman does not want to wear the headgear, it's ok, it's alright, but all her headgear-wearing sisters will avoid her like the plague, making her life impossible and her position untenable. Those who have no talent, skill nor education and refuse to wear the headgear will be labeled as sluts, whores and unclean heathens until they submit. Submit! Or leave! That is our slogan, our battle cry.

"Errr, sorry, wait, wait. Actually that was last year's slogan, last year's theme. This year we have a new one, more in keeping with out seminal priorities. Do you want to hear it, brothers and sisters?"

"Yes!"

"This year, our slogan, our mantra, our theme is 'Born to Haram!'"

"This is not extremism cutting off the path; no, rather, it lights the path for us, it lights the path for those who can see, those who believe, those who want to believe, those people who cannot and will not be corrupted. They, the abject moderates and the shameless secularists, want to drown out the call, the call that unites us all, the call that will save us from damnation.

"Our code, system, rule of law and style of governance is comprehensive. There is no discrimination between the sexes and there is no discrimination between us and the banana-leaf users or the chopstick operators.

"What we say goes and what they say goes as well, as long as it is neither important nor threatening. If it is important we'll ignore it and pretend to give the matter some thought. If we are pushed or forced to take action and to make a decision when we don't want to, we'll turn it over to our youth wing and their vigilante mobs and paramilitary squads led by militant leaders who are answerable to no policeman, lawyer or judge; they only have to answer to our learned collection of Supreme Council members.

"I am aware this contradicts my previous statement on the matter of the law-abiding behaviour of Party officials and Party members, but there it is, so get used to it.

"Tourists need not worry. We'll only defend ourselves against other locals and there is no truth to the rumour that foreigners will be attacked, kidnapped and held to ransom as a way to fund the building of religious schools.

The Boss Teacher stopped and smiled a thin, watery smile. He couldn't drink any water, it was fasting month, so he took a deep breath and continued, "Brothers, I return to the subject that is close and dear to our hearts, one of the pillars of our campaign platform, one of the tenets of our vision - the timely and necessary reformation of the civil service and the introduction of a practice which has no precedent in the history of Western civilization – that is the hiring of plain or wretchedly ugly women will be given preference over the employment of stunning, beautiful or cute females, reason being a beautiful woman will inevitably marry well and secure a comfortable life for herself, her family, her relatives and friends.

"Our Party says let's give the ordinary women of this nation a chance, a chance to work and an opportunity to contribute. It is a well known fact that the lack of temptation contributes to an efficient and productive workplace. As any dirty old man and filthy young man knows it is easier to work if you are not horny.

"Beautiful women belong in the bedroom, not behind a desk. They should be on their backs looking at the ceiling, not sitting up typing. They should collect jewellery, handbags and shoes, wear make-up and smell great. Think about it, you men, if the ugly females are busy all the time, what with working in an office, and cooking, cleaning and ironing at home, that will leave them too tired to monitor and control their husbands' necessary movements.

"We will lower the legal age for marriage to 15 years and three months for girls and 15 years and two weeks for boys. Families will be created by the thousands, forming a strong moral foundation and creating a consumer society which will drive the economy through over-spending on children and taking out loans for weddings, for houses, for cars, for travel and so on. A lower age-limit for marriage will also mean men will enjoy the benefit of being married to a lively, frisky, speedy teenager. A satisfactory conjugal existence will remove the desire or need for an unsavoury, unseemly, torrid and illicit extra-marital office romance, affair or fling , and help dim or erase thoughts of lust, envy and vanity thus allowing co-workers to prosper and thrive in a happy and harmonious workplace,"

"I hope the days of Women's Groups and NGO's mildly protesting and meekly complaining about whichever of our policies they deem fit to question are over. They should instead teach their mis-directed fussy flock to be practiced experts in their universal and crucial responsibility, which is until further notice, the miracle of childbirth.

"So I ask these women, these feminists and sisters; what more do you want? What more do you need? Rights? You are allowed to work and encouraged to have babies. You are allowed to go anywhere, unescorted, in all sorts of dress at any time of day or night with no relatives in sight, which as you may well know brethren, is practically an impossibility in our brother country Afghanistan.

"Women in Malaysia are allowed to vote, which is not the case in our brother country Kuwait; in some places in our country women can even vote more than once, but they should not vote more often than men, that would be unladylike.

"Women and girls are allowed to drive cars, noisy motorbikes and cute little scooters anytime, anywhere which, as you know brethren, is forbidden in the Kingdom of Saudi Arabia.

"On top of that if the women of Malaysia wish to travel overseas, they do not need the permission of their husbands which, unfortunately, is how it always is in Egypt. The final point, my brave and loyal subjects, is that we in Malaysia do not go round killing our sisters, nieces, cousins and aunties where every two weeks or so, the thought of the day that presents itself to gentlemen of a certain ilk and of an unfortunate disposition is 'I'm going to cut you into little pieces.'

"Yes, there are always exceptions to the rule, but we have to be fair. Men have to carry the load, that's why they get all the breaks. Sisters … surely four wives are a small reward for a lifetime of endeavour, humiliation and eating salt? That is how it was written!"

A murmur of assent arose from the gathering.

"We, our Party, we have the Truth. It is our duty to share it with you, whether you like it or not."

The crowd rose to cheer and raised their clenched fists. A man next to me said, "Truly, we are blessed to have such a wise and learned leader, and truly does our leader demonstrate awesome clarity and dignity."

The Boss Teacher waved his arms, and his flock fell to silence.

"Now I would like to clear up one or two details, technicalities apropos flogging. Yes, kind souls; the punishment of man to instill and infuse the fear of God. Without fear of God, man is but a beast in the concrete jungle. The reason the world is in such a miserable and terrible state is because we no longer believe in the wrath of God. We refuse to see the signs around us. We are desensitized to world-wide suffering and torment. We refuse to consider a higher power at work. A Power that is ashamed and displeased. We no longer believe in Hell.

Science and greed have conspired to diminish God. These sinners say He can not be proven, therefore we should not be afraid of Him. God has been usurped by money, by selfishness, by power. Only when we are about to die do we ask for forgiveness. Only then do we cry out our repentance. All the money in the world cannot stay the hand of death. Yes, brothers and sisters, look around you, Man seeks to create Heaven on earth, as if such a thing were possible.

"It is our duty to show men a sample of Hell; a glimpse. To bring Hell to earth. So that you can feel it, see it, taste it, smell it and dream of it. The laws do not suffice. They are hopelessly inadequate, and protect the rich, the powerful and the fortunate.

"We will return to the laws of our ancestors. To a time when the world was pure and chaste. To an age when the fear of God was as real and concrete as a pebble in your palm. When our Party comes to power, you will see with your own eyes and hear with your own ears flogging and stoning.

"Barbarianism? Or a cheap and unforgettable deterrent? You be the judge, brothers. We have devised an all-encompassing system for punishment. Our departments of marketing, research and polling have been hard at work devising a formula that is acceptable to at least seventy-percent of our electorate. We are pleased that this new system of punishment, new to this country, but ancient historically, has polled very well, particularly in the 50-80 age bracket. That stands to reason, for they are the ones who have eaten the most salt, whose minds contain wisdom gained from experience.

"How crime and punishment shall be attended to and enforced by the Party, your future government, with the mandate of the electorate, and of every sensible and God fearing voter, is as follows: corruption … two hundred lashes, then buried in the ground, up to the neck, then stoned for two hours with no rock larger than a fist or heavier than a kilo. Stoning will stop once the prisoner is pronounced dead. If the prisoner is still alive his left hand will be amputated. The procedure shall take place in an ambulance and the public are not allowed to be witnesses to the event. Or shake or bang on the ambulance. The police shall respond in no uncertain terms if you do so.

"Embezzlement … two hundred lashes, then buried to the waist, stoned for one hour; if still alive after all that, the left hand to be cut off.

The audience started to clap.

"No applause, please, this is not a game show. I ask for reflection and solemnity."

The crowd looked at their feet and shuffled them.

"Nepotism … two hundred lashes, buried to the waist, stoned for an hour, no amputation. We understand why sinners would like to keep their money in the family, it is only natural. Some of them might have more than one, and thus have more reason for avarice.

"Now, my dear brothers and sisters, there is a qualifier; that, while punishment is open to all members of the public, even children, for what is a better deterrent than for children to see what might happen to them if they transgress, stoning, amputations and beheadings are not, I repeat, not open to women. Amputations and beheadings are for VIPs only. Stoning is for men.

"It is forbidden for any woman even if she knows the prisoner or was the victim of the crime. Any woman who pretends to be a man so as to participate in the stoning will herself be stoned until she is no longer sensible or conscious. Any man who pretends to be a woman for whatever ludicrous reason will be dealt with later in this sermon.

"Why, you ask, why deny women the right to stone someone to death? My answer is this; women are too fragile and precious to be subjected to such displays of vengeance and brutality. Imagine, brothers and sisters, the scene of a stoning … the skull fractures, the nose-breaks, blood gushing from eye-sockets, issuing from the nose, mouth and ears, blood-sprays.

"With lashings, all you see are welts and a trickle of blood here and there. Many of you dear sisters have whipped your children. That does not mean that we, the Party, respect you any less. What you will see, that nightmarish scene, may cause some of you to find it hard to sleep at night which may lead to disharmony in the bed.

"We cannot allow that. We cannot risk it. Women must be protected from the base, gross and gory aspects of life. Their hearts must be pure, their eyes shielded, their ears covered like their hair and sexy bits. It is a fact that women cannot handle excitement, titillation or degradation; a woman's heart is weak, she faints easily. Who's ever heard of a man fainting? Who has ever heard of a group of boys going into hysterics?

"We revere and adore women. That is why we do not allow them to be horrified, shocked and appalled."

Warm applause filled the sultry air. The Boss Teacher mopped his face with a white handkerchief.

"To continue in detail God's punishment as installed by His servants working for the glory of, and Party of, God; I proclaim, for the crime of Adultery … one hundred lashes if the partner is unmarried, three hundred lashes if the partner in crime and sin is. After said lashes, buried in earth up to the neck, to be stoned for one hour or until the prisoner is dead. If the prisoner is still alive, her or she shall be released, hopefully a repentant soul.

"Next, homosexuality - this applies to men only. We do not punish lesbians, we know not what to do with them, except to return them to their families and have them do as they see fit. However, we are upset that they will not provide us with babies. For babies are the front line in the eternal war with the infidel.

"Male homosexuals are to be given two hundred and fifty lashes, then buried to the waist, stoned for three hours or until they are dead. If they are still alive after said punishment both arms shall be amputated and they will be thrown into the sea. Our land is too good for them and they shall not rot in it.

"Bisexuals will be lashed three hundred times, buried to the waist, then stoned for four hours or until they are dead.

After that, we will behead them and throw the corpse into the sea. Bisexuality is an abomination beyond the pale. I regret that bisexuals only have one life to give.

"I predict a significant drop in AIDS and sexually transmitted diseases, and homosexuals and bisexuals, once we gain power and our system of justice becomes the law of the land. How any person in their right mind could find that objectionable I cannot understand for the life of me. Surely the people will rejoice and give thanks to such wisdom that makes our beloved country better, safer and more livable for themselves, their families and their many children. Those that are pure, chaste and loyal have nothing to fear, but those who are decadent, sick and depraved … your time is over.

"We are going to take the country back and we don't care how many we have to kill to do it. You will be wiped out, I promise, and believe me, you will not be missed. No one will visit your grave, no one will pray for you, nor shed tears.

"Alcoholism … alcoholics shall be given one hundred lashes, stoned for an hour, helmet allowed, both hands amputated and their tongues cut off so that they cannot tell anyone anymore stories. Personally, I despise alcoholics. They never shut up. They talk too much and are always full of ideas and plans. Ideas and plans forgotten and discarded the next morning in the cold sober light of day.

"They feel it incumbent upon themselves to explain what is wrong with the world, yet they are unable to see what is wrong with them selves. Worst of all, they don't care. An alcoholic always thinks he is right, always thinks he is clever. The arrogance of an alcoholic is second to none.

"The stupidity of an alcoholic is second to none. He believes he has no fear, but that belief is temporary. Take away his alcohol and you take away his wings. Then his ideas dry up and his lips are sealed. But come Happy Hour, and there he goes again, thinking he's better than us, and mouthing off to anyone within earshot. To people that never asked his opinion in the first place, and do not want to hear his latest diatribe. But he wants to prove that he's better than all of us, smarter, funnier. But nothing will ever come of it, because an alcoholic cannot be trusted to finish the job. To follow through with the plan. To put into practice the great idea. He will forever be a loser, because that is what alcoholics are. More importantly, an alcoholic can never be trusted to tell the truth. Cut off their tongues. That will do society a big favour."

"Drug addiction. Brothers and Sisters, unlike the present government we do not use one term or word to refer to all drugs. We are more specific, that is to say, we are aware of the difference between hard and soft drugs, between that which is created by man and that created by God.

"We know that God believes in the details, unlike the heathens of the West who believe, erroneously, that the Devil lies in the details. Silly buggers. All drugs are not created equal, just as all men are not created equal, an obvious and glaring example being the stupidity of the present government as opposed to the wisdom of our Party.

"Let's start with syabu, commonly known as ice, scientifically known as methamphetamine. The punishment for users, pushers and manufacturers is as follows: two hundred and fifty lashes, then buried to the neck with no helmet allowed, and stoned for twelve hours; after which the corpse shall be beheaded and the carcass thrown into the jungle to be eaten by any beast who is interested in a skinny rake of a body.

"We believe that syabu is the drug of the Devil. Yes, brothers and sisters, the Devil made this drug and is destroying the world with it. Our rising crime rate can be linked directly to the widespread use of this abomination.

"Now we turn to Ecstasy ... the second most heinous drug to have infected our society. Ecstasy makes one dance and dance and dance. And we know women by nature love to dance. But dancing of that sort must be forbidden; it is too sexy, far too vulgar for our eastern sensibilities, our pious roots, our modest values. Haram haram haram! We were born to haram. Because ecstasy leads to dancing and dancing leads to sex and sex leads to loose women and loose women will lead to the destruction of the family.

"So anyone caught doing Ecstasy will receive 88 lashes, then be buried up to the waist and be stoned for half an hour, helmet allowed, after which he or she will be sent to rehab for one year and three months. We do not wish to kill all the young people in Kuala Lumpur. Recidivists shall be sent to Lumut for two years. If that doesn't work, nothing will.

"Cocaine ... all cocaine users shall be denied the use of their credit cards, and put into rehab for two years. The second time they break the law, they will be whipped 50 times and sent to Kuching and placed under house arrest for three years, without the possibility of getting a pardon from any member of royalty that might be on good terms with said prisoner.

"Kuching is even more boring than Kota Baru or Raub, so you can imagine the torment the prisoner has to endure. We still need them to contribute to society for they are probably the best and brightest among the younger generation.

"Heroin, morphine and amphetamine sulphate. I don't have to say too much about these users; there is the needle and the damage done, once you have crossed that line, your life is worthless because obviously you do not care if you live or die.

"So we'll finish the job for them. Two hundred lashes, then buried up to the neck, stoned for two hours, and if the prisoner is still alive, he or she shall be beheaded, cremated and the ashes scattered to the wind.

"Ganja. Yes, brothers, ganja or marijuana, also known as grass, weed, reefer, blunt, joint, spliff, stuff, t-shirt, dapur, barang, ubat and balut was created by God. That is an undeniable fact. It is part of nature, millions of years old. Our brothers in Acheh have been growing, smoking and selling it for centuries. Thus, we find it too difficult to be too harsh on ganja users. What's good for our brothers in arms is good enough for us, you might say. Nevertheless, 20 lashes and we'll drop you back after it's over.

"Cough medicine, 20 lashes and your motorcycle licence will be suspended for a year. The second time you are caught, no bike-riding for life.

"If you have any questions or queries, please visit our website at borntoharam.com or contact your local representative.

"Turning to other, somewhat lighter matters, we understand that young people in this day and age need an outlet, an atmosphere in which to relax and have a bit of fun. Yes, brothers, fun. We are not cold nor insensitive to the desires of the young or the young at heart. We remember what it is like to be young. Some of us know what it is like to be very young. It is our duty to present our charitable side. God demands it.

"And we are happy to acquiesce … brothers, sisters and children, we propose to stage a model concert, free from degradation and vice, free from corruption and base sexuality, free from the influence of the infidel West. A concert that is at once spiritually, physically and morally healthy.

"It is not true we are against entertainment. We are not against entertainment per se, just elements associated with it which are contrary to the beliefs we hold to be sacred.

"We are fond of group singing, that is, groups of boys and groups of girls, standing, swaying some of the time, but no dancing and swaying of the hips. There is no tolerance on hip-shaking.

"Then a male soloist will perform, followed by a female soloist. They will then do a duet, and will keep a respectable distance apart, absolutely no touching allowed. After which a traditional dance shall be presented that will be free of any suggestion of homosexuality.

"A display of martial arts exhibited by the best talented exponents in the country will then follow. This will consume at least 20 minutes, most of which will be taken up by the exponents circling each other, slapping their thighs and yelling for no apparent reason."

The crowd cheered, whistled and stamped their feet. The Boos Teacher smiled, spread his arms, soaked in sweat, applause and adulation.

"There will be a dinner and dialogue this Saturday at the Hotel Malaya. It will start at 7 pm. Please don't be late because it will be held against you. Prayers will start at 7.15 p.m. Dinner will be served at 7.45. I will begin speaking at 8 p.m. We will have a recess at 8.30 for prayers which should finish at 9.30. I will then continue speaking until 11 p.m., after which a light supper will be served. Smoking is not allowed in the ballroom, so some of you might take this opportunity to get some fresh air.

"At 11.15 our brother Boss Teacher, a great Boss Teacher if you ask me, a superb orator and an immensely wise and learned man from our neighbouring state of Terengganu, Boss Teacher Abu Bakar, my deputy and the future leader of our Party shall then take the podium and speak for an hour, reaffirming everything I said previously, but with a flourish, with flair, and with fire.

"In the spirit of unity we will invite other guests such as the lame-duck leaders of minor opposition parties, affectionately known as our coalition partners. Parti Socialis Malaysia shall not be invited because they are atheists and have only six members.

"Women's groups and non-governmental organizations shall also be ignored because they are of no use to society and are powerless. They are akin to dogs chained to a fence barking all day long at anyone that happens to pass by. A nuisance full of sound and fury signifying nothing and accomplishing less.

"Brothers, sisters, ladies and gentlemen, God bless you, God bless us, God bless the Party and God bless our country."

I made my way toward the stalls. I would surprise mother and bring home the best of what fasting month had to offer, a gastronomic treasure once a year for thirty days.

The longest queue by far was for Penang popia. The name of the stall was naturally "No. 1." I went to school with the grandson. I went to school with the fish lady's son too. This was our town before we were swamped by thousands of immigrants who couldn't speak a word of English. But I digress. It wasn't their fault. They needed to come where the money was.

However, they could have learned some manners instead of spitting all over the place and staring like dogs at Chinese girls in skirts, and right after Friday prayers too. Just because you prayed on Friday doesn't mean you can stare at anyone and spit on anything, like you own the streets, like you own the day, especially when you just moved in yesterday. Still I digress.

I didn't bother with the kind of food you could find anywhere the rest of the year. I was looking for Raya food. Roti jala, called roti sorai in Penang; ayam percik, five bucks a piece, sotong bakar and ikan bakar, usually pari, stingray ... the same couple ran the stall for years, the guy called me "brother." Nasi kerabu, blue rice, the blue of Manchester City and Coventry, with salted fish, paru, bean sprouts, keropok, coconut and cili padi. Add a drumstick and you pay three bucks.

"Nasi tomato, red rice like the red on the cheeks of a Japanese child, with ayam masak merah and begedel,, three eighty and you have cucumber and pineapple too. Laksa Johor and soto (my mother's favourite), pasembor (also from Penang, more elegant and literate than rojak), desserts filled with gula Mekaka and shredded coconut, spicy hors d'oeuvres with tiny salted prawns.

The drink stalls parade pink (Bandung), green (sugar cane), yellow (corn) and black (mata kucing). Clear would be lime, red will be rose and I have no idea what that lavender one is.

I like curry puffs with potato, beef and sardines and that spicy deep fried disk with a prawn and coconut filling. My mother loves pulut udang, our version of sushi, but with a spicy centre. I have no use for porridge, the favourite dish of our Prime Minister. Our first Prime Minister ate ikan bawal with cili padi and rice. Therein lies the difference.

I bought nasi kerabu, nasi tomato, soto, pulut udang, roti sorai and a fine-sized pari (for seven bucks, a dollar discount, for old times' sake), kuih lapis and a kambing murtabak. I could see my mother shaking her head, saying, "It's too much, it's too much." And feign irritation and complaining about the cost, but she'd be happy.

As I walked home, I thought, if some people have souls, they must keep it well hidden.

By the way, I almost forgot, I bought two dollars worth of kuih cara. Do you know kuih cara? The small green circular cake with little brown spots on the top, and is flat at the base, like a sphere cut in two. It has gula melaka in the middle. That's the one that as you bite it, you have to keep your mouth shut, because it explodes.

this bar is called heaven

....

Been away, now I'm back. I don't suppose it would be possible to write like Faulkner. William Faulkner. It would have to be a solitary life.

There is no way Kawabata can be approached. One could try to copy something of his style, but it would be false, hollow; unless you had a childhood of loneliness and sadness. He was born in it. Had it coursing through his veins. Miniaturization is a part of their apotheosis, part of their culture. The haiku, the bonsai, the silicon chip. Kawabata is style incarnate. His technique unsettles and laughs loudly in your face.

Then there is Lawrence, Woolfe, and Joyce. One can see Joyce and Kawabata getting together for a drink. They would have lots to say, and probably wouldn't even argue. Virginia Woolfe, sulking and scowling, would be at the bar alone.

At the table next to the window, sit Somerset Maugham, Forster, and Isherwood. Now that would be the place to be! Fast and furious, no doubt, full of humour, wit and compassion.

Oh, oh, trouble brews, look who's just walked in alone and unshaven - Ernest Hemingway, and he's in his 'Green Hills of Africa' mood, better stay away. He glares at the trio by the window, moves to the bar. Virginia Woolfe takes one look at him and cuts him dead, then takes another sip.

Ernest sits at the other end of the bar.

"Where are Henry and Scott today?"

The bartender replies, "Mr.Fitzgerald has been taken ill, and Mr.Miller is at the beach."

'Why do I even ask?' thinks Ernest.

Kawabata and Joyce sit in silence. Maugham, Forster, and Isherwood never stop talking. Actually Maugham and Forster would take turns holding centre-stage and Isherwood would sit quietly and note it all down. Forster is a kind man who likes everybody. He praises Isherwood's latest book and buys a scotch for Virginia. Normally he'd go over and say hello, but she's had a rough time lately, and he's sure she'd rather be left alone.

The bartender complains about Dostoyevsky's bill, which has been unpaid for months. It's hard to turn down the Russian when he is drunk. I mean ... he is who he is. The bartender asks Ernest whether he could settle Dostoyevsky's bill.

"You want me to settle that crazy Russian's bill? Are you crazy? Lemme see anyway."

Ernest pays for a couple of weeks off Dostoyevsky's bill. "There still a lot there, but at least it's something," he thinks. "Next time he comes in, I'll wring his neck!"

Forster, who likes Ernest as well, buys a double scotch for him. Ernest, who can't stand charity, drinks it anyway. Maugham is talking about painting, Kawabata is thinking about autumn, and Joyce remembers the quiet sobs of a night long past.

A few minutes later, the French arrive. Jean-Paul Sartre and Albert Camus come through the door and they immediately grab everyone's attention. They have a message from their friend Andre Gide. "He is traveling" says Jean-Paul, "and begs us to pass on this message to you incurable and irretrievable pub dwellers."

Ernest manages a smile; the English by the window look at the Frenchmen expectantly.

"The message is," continues Camus, "nothing thwarts happiness so much as the memory of happiness."

"If only that would apply to sadness." replies Ernest, whereupon Kawabata and Joyce nod their heads vigorously. Forster is so moved he buys a round of scotch for everyone.

the licence

••••

I have been here almost four and a half months. I've seen snow, sun, rain and heard hail. What I have not seen are fences, walls, gates, barbed wire rusting over shards of glass embedded and sealed in cement.

All my life I have looked at gates, when I was young looking through and beyond them, later looking over them, but still trying to look for any signs of life. A dog perhaps, or a maid hanging clothes on a line.

Here there are none. Not around an un-insulated, bare, square wooden house, such as the one we live in nor around houses with flower beds, French windows and entrances for every member of the family. I'd be terrified to be alone in a gorgeous house with so many windows and the kitchen door, the garage door, the patio doors, the cat door and the front door to worry about.

I'd never watch TV with the sound up nor listen to music on headphones for fear of not hearing the time-stopping crunch of footsteps uninvited or the squeak of the window in the guest bathroom. The fact that I would give my soul to live in a house with a guest bathroom does not enter into it. I'd have to get a weapon. And when I bought one, three would follow. "I need two guns for upstairs and two for downstairs, OK!?" Leaves only had to rustle in a black sky and bang I'd shoot and down would drop poor Mr. Fuzzy.

I want to get used to living in a place with no fences, no walls, no gates, no broken jagged triangles of glass to remind one of the evil beyond the gates. We live five or six blocks from downtown Lafayette across the Wabash River, from West Lafayette and the campus of Purdue.

Christine and I went to the courthouse to get our marriage licence. There were more security guards than people in there. We removed everything from our pockets and walked through a metal detector. I wore a dark green shirt and black trousers frayed at the heels and Christine wore a Buffalo Sabers t-shirt and white shorts. There was a very old iron elevator with doors and a big wheel at the side of it. The marriage licence office was on the second floor. Christine wanted to try it, I said no. I wasn't going to take an elevator, no matter how quaint it was, to go up just one floor.

The counter was chest high. A young man with a large tattoo on his right forearm listened to Christine and asked for photo-identification. He had a detached look about him like any student who had to work whilst in school. He spoke very softly and looked at his computer screen. Christine was radiant. I didn't know what to do with my hands. He looked at my passport and then at Christine's driver's licence and started typing. He asked me where I was born. I told him. He apologized because it said so on my passport. Christine giggled.

He asked me what my occupation was and Christine said, "He's unemployed," and stammered because what she meant to say was I was not working yet and that's why we are getting married so that I can get a Green Card but that's not the reason why we are getting married, it's just the reason I'm unemployed. The man shrugged and pouted to suggest it did not matter to him one way or another; he was just filling in the blanks and supposed to ask what our occupations were. I said "writer".

He looked at me, "A writer?" "Yeah." He nodded and and typed it. Only old people laugh at artists. They only want to know one thing, how are you going to make money. Like as though we want to marry their ugly daughters. How did YOU make your money old man? Whose position did you undermine, how long did you have to kiss ass? Who did you stab in the back and pretend it never happened?

"Father's first name?"

"Leslie."

"Last name?" I told him.

"And where does he live?"

"He has passed away."

"Mother's first name?" I told him.

"And where does she live?" He typed it.

It was Christine's turn.

"Where were you born?"

"In the U.S."

"What state?"

"Indiana."

"Occupation?"

"Err, just put general labour."

Christine was truthful and modest. She was a quality control line supervisor at her last job. Now she is at Toyota. She got the job because her resume was impressive. It is only a matter of time before she'd be promoted to quality control. She studied architecture and was almost a paramedic, but she couldn't hack the injuries and the blood. She also paints, carves, writes and had edited and designed a magazine. She'd tell me one 'c' and two 'esses' if I asked her about 'necessary'. My spelling is appalling.

"Father's first name?"

"Dennis."

"Last name?" Christine told him.

"And where does he live?"

"He's deceased."

"Mother's first name?"

"Phyllis."

"I never know how to spell Phyllis. Is that with two 'ls'? Christine laughed and said yes.

"And there does she live?"

"Illinois." He typed it.

"Actually, wait, err, she's also deceased."

"Oh, are you sure?" Delete.

Her father had passed away, but her mother was alive. I didn't ask her about it later. Christine was brought up by her grandparents. They had legally adopted her. Now they were both dead and when her father died, she had no family left.

"Have you ever been married?" When he asked me I said no, I'd never even been engaged.

"Yes," Christine said.

"Divorced or deceased?"

"Divorced."

"Any children?"

"No."

"OK, I have to ask you questions that you both have to answer. Are you under the influence of alcohol or drugs at this moment?"

"No." "No."

"Have you ever been arrested and convicted?"

"No." "No."

"Do you have any communicable diseases such as …"

"No." "No."

"Are you related by blood any closer than second cousins?" Christine giggled.

"No." "No."

"OK, you have to read this and sign here and here."

It was one page with a line in the middle and a metal clip at the top. Christine signed and I did too, with a steady hand.

"This pink slip has the names of the judges who will perform the ceremony. You can contact them to schedule an appointment."

She pulled out a slip and the title was 'Officials Who Perform Wedding Ceremonies.' Underneath it said: The following are people who will perform wedding ceremonies. To schedule an appointment, you need to contact their office at the listed number. Fees should be discussed when you make the appointment.

Christine took out the twenty for the marriage licence. He printed the receipt and the marriage licence and marriage certificate with our names on it, middle initials included.

He also gave us the state of Indiana original marriage certificate which was blank and a marriage licence form which was titled HOW TO OBTAIN A CERTIFIED COPY OF YOUR MARRIAGE LICENCE which we were to complete and return along with a US$2 money order (DO NOT SEND CASH) and a business-sized, self-addressed stamped envelope to:

Tippecanoe County Clerk,
PO Box 1665,
310 Main Str, Courthouse,
Lafayette, IN 47902

There was also a blue slip titled: Tippecanoe County Clerk of Courts. Under the address and number, it read: "The person performing the Marriage Ceremony must fill out and return BOTH pages of the original Marriage Licence and Record of Marriage to the Tippecanoe County Clerk's Office, OO Box 1665, Lafayette, IN 47902. An envelope is provided to the Bride and Groom at the time of the application. The Place and Date of Marriage MUST be completed."

"A certified copy of the Marriage Licence will be mailed to you as soon as the Marriage Licence and Record of Marriage have been received from you. If you have any questions or comments, you may contact us," the young man putting all the documents into a white, unmarked envelope. He also gave us two brochures, one titled: "Money Skills for Newlywed Couples" from the office of the Indiana Secretary of State (Securities Division), the other "Before You Marry" – infomation about sexually transmitted diseases and HIV.

Christine asked, "Why would they give information on STDs now? Isn't it too late?"

"That's precisely what I keep saying, but we have to give this out, so there you go."

It was over in fifteen minutes. We walked out of the courthouse with a marriage licence. Yes, we'd have to come back, but no one could or would turn us away.

They'd even provide us with two witnesses. The licence was Monday and the ceremony is going to be on Friday.

Christine and I lived in my country for eight months. If we were to be married there she'd have to convert to Islam. Christine is Catholic. I have a great deal of respect for Catholics. JFK was a Catholic. The great Irish writers were Catholic. Evelyn Waugh converted to Catholicism.

The only reason I am a Muslim is because when my parents divorced I lived with my mother. According to her, my father was a Methodist. An Indian Methodist. I have often wondered what it would have been like to have been raised a Methodist. My cousins on my father's side are terrific. Honest, straightforward, direct and warm. They laugh often and tease.

I wasn't given a chance to choose my religion, my mother is Muslim and that was that. I gave up on Islam when I was fourteen. The only prayer I memorized was: "Our Father, who art in heaven" – Al-Fatiha.

Now, I cannot remember it. Perhaps I never understood it. I don't speak Arabic and I have no idea what the words mean. I was forced to memorize it, like I was forced to memorize my prayers; if there was a translation, I could not be bothered with it. It was a chore that had to be done. I forgot my prayers because I never prayed. There was nothing to pray for. There was no one to pray with.

I am half Indian and half Malay but I am neither and belong to no one. Though it is true, in school, I could play football for either the Malay side or the non-Malay side, and I did, switching teams whenever I was needed. So to ask Christine to convert when I had wanted to get out since I was fourteen is out of the question. I am not interested in scoring points for Islam or for my god-forsaken soul. And having strangers advising Christine on how to be a good and proper Muslim would have been intolerable. I would have had to take classes and recite prayers, prayers in a language I know zero of and care about even less. Now if I could have prayed in English, that would have been a different matter, but there are no miracles in this stinking world.

My darling Christine and I are getting married this Friday, on the 8th of August, 2008. 8/8/08. My Chinese friends doubtless know the significance of the numbers and the date. Triple Eight. I'm not sure what it means. Triple Happiness? Triple Good Luck? Triple Auspiciousness? Whatever it is, it's a good number.

the wind chill factor

••••

"Hey Marco, dude, wake up buddy, we gotta get to the distributor. C'mon man it's 6.30, we gotta get in line dude. Marco, beer. Drink beer, keg of beer."

I shot up; frozen and prehistoric. Tomo had kicked the bed and slapped my legs and rushed out of the room, his winter jacket rustling in the cold.

"C'mon Marco, we gotta go, we gotta go. Jefro's waiting in the car man."

Washing a frozen face with freezing water didn't seem to make much sense to me, but I did it anyway. I kicked the bathroom door to let Tomo know I was up. I grabbed my black knee-length overcoat and put on my Dr. Martens.

Tomo was waiting for me in the corridor. He was grinning. "How are you doing buddy? Hope I didn't wake you up. What time did you crash?"

"About 2.30."

"That's not too bad."

"Not too bad for Maggie Thatcher maybe, but 4 hours is painful."

"You'll get plenty of sleep when you're dead, Marco."

"I'm looking forward to it."

"You'd better be."

"Is the engine warm?"

"Yeah, it's running, heater's running too."

Tomo pushed the door open with both hands; a blast of winter greeted us.

I shut my eyes. Tomo was in the passenger seat. Jefro was driving and had fake I.D. I brought my passport along just in case, actually I carried my passport everywhere. Its shape was curved because it lived in the back pocket of my jeans. I used cellophane tape to hold that thing together.

"What can I do for you gentlemen today?"

Jefro said," A quarter keg of Old Mill please, and a case of Miller's Genuine Draft. Does John want ponies?"

"Yes," answered Tomo and I.

"And a case of Rolling Rock ponies."

"That'll be 54.95. Drive on up there and we'll be right out."

We crawled out of the distributor's. It was Tomo's car, but if there were no girls he let Jefro drive it so he could crank up the stereo and bounce and punch and scream.

The view was snow and ice; dirty brown and grey slush in the gutters, pristine crunching white on the pavements, soft glinting icing in the trees.

The Miller Draft botttles were twist-offs. I declined the offer, preferring to wait for the moment, the ritualistic, unifying sanctity of the keg being tapped, the cup of foam, the cool beer.

"Hey Marco, are you sleeping back there you wuss?"

"No, I'm listening to the music."

"Well, suit yourself. I'm going for a hit."

"You brought the bowl? Alright! There is a God. Why the fuck didn't you tell me man?"

"Cause you were being such a wuss. I gotta get you up. I gotta wait for you."

"You didn't wait five fucking minutes man."

"Bullshit."

"I was scraping ice off the windshield for about 15 minutes," said Jefro.

"Yeah, fuckin' A man."

"Alright, alright, pass me the bowl, lecture over mommy and daddy."

"You're gonna wait your fuckin' turn," said Tomo.

"Paterno says we're not ready. Paterno says we'll be ready next year," said John.

"Sure, they'll be Seniors next year," said Rich.

"But he always says that, he always says the same thing. He doesn't want to sound off like some jerk, like the rest of 'em. He never says we're gonna win, no matter who we play. It's always they're a tough team, they're a good school, they've got some good kids, our kids are ok, but they're not that great, not quite ready, but you know he's ready to kick some ass, oh yeah. He doesn't like to shoot his mouth off, that's all."

Today was Saturday - college football game day. This was a place called Happy Valley, with a stadium named Beaver, in a town called State College and our Lions were called Nittany, on account of Mount Nittany nearby, which was nowhere near a mountain, more like a hill. This was Penn State. A bumpersticker in front of us read, "If God isn't a Penn State fan, why is the sky blue and white?"

You got me there.

We were in town now, there were cables low over the intersection, traffic lights hanging by a thread, hung in threes; stop signs, road signs, signs for dealerships, gas stations, restaurants, streamers tied from the sidewalks to the entrance, price reductions in the windows.

"Do you wanna get something to eat Marko?" asked Tomo.

"Yeah, cold pizza and warm beer."

"No, no, fuck that, let's get something good to eat."

A voice on the radio intoned, country-wise and avuncular, "I have a very appetizing proposition to make, but please don't eat your radio. The proposition, two succulent hot dogs, plump and meaty, tender and sizzling, not one but two all-beef hotdogs on a special twin bun you'll only find in one place, your A-Plus mini-market. They call it the Double Dog, and they sell this mouth-thrilling belly- filling feast for just 89 cents. If you find this proposition tempting, I suggest you proceed in an orderly fashion to your nearest A-Plus mini-market and devour a twin bun double dog." (The emphasis on 'devour' was almost obscene.) The jingle ran, "Get the plus, A Plus, get the plus, A Plus."

Tomo laughed. "I'm sick of hot dogs. I'm fuckin' sick of fucking pizzas and I'm sick of Chicken Cosmos."

I defended my favourite. "Hey, man, don't lump Cosmos with that shit. I love Chicken Cosmos, best chicken sandwich in the free world. What about Subway? Submarine?" I appealed.

"Not fuckin' open yet, Marko you shit," said Tomo.

"Coffee for three," said Tomo. Tomo had pancakes and Jefro ordered cinnamon rolls which he split with me. I ordered scrambled eggs, hash browns and sausages.

There was constant mopping of the floors and wiping off table tops. The waitresses wore thick black skirts of varying lengths, stiff white shirts with hard collars with the sleeves rolled up, and with their hair tied back. Ye Olde College Diner was long and narrow, with wooden booths with hooks for hanging your coat and high wooden panels for privacy. This establishment remained open 24 hours and served hot breakfast throughout.

We left a tip and stepped out to the light of winter in our eyes. Now we were ready to drink beer, liquor and red wine and lose our voices for Penn State, especially since it was Notre Dame and the game was on ABC with Keith Jackson and we were unbeaten.

The DJ knew the caller. "ZOO 92, can I help you?"

"Yeah, man."

"What's happening with you man?"

"Oh, not much man, the cat's trying to play with the telephone, man, and I'm getting peeved."

"What's the cat's name?"

"Muff."

"Buff, you've got a cat named Muff?"

"Yeah, Buff and Muff, you know, damn, he keeps messing with the phone, man. I get, yeah, peeved with him."

"Buff, I didn't think you were the kind of individual who likes cats."

"I love cats, man. I used to have one in 'Nam."

"I knew a guy who had a cat in 'Nam, but it was for Thanksgiving Dinner."

"Well yes, we used to do that." A two six-pack a day laugh cracked on the radio.

"Yeah, I heard some horror stories about that place."

"Yeah really, I don't really want to talk about that."

"Yeah, let's get off the flashback. Let's start talking about some rock n' roll. What d'you wanna hear?"

"Well, I was thinking about some Alan Parsons today."

"Well, how about something from 'Eve' or something like that?"

"Yeah, something really beautiful."

"Music that makes you feel good, not old, Central Pennsylvania's home of Rock 'n Roll, ZOO 92."

My first roomate at Penn State was a Marine. He was wide of girth, with beard and moustache and smiling eyes just this side of okay. He looked like a biker.

"Do you drink beer?"

I said yes, though I preferred vodka and whiskey. He opened a tiny fridge and it was full of Rolling Rock. We were going to be friends. Sharing beer is uncommon among students because nobody buys two six-packs for himself, but the Marine was older and used to cases. He did not give a damn.

He called me his "Iranian hostage" and we got along fine. He'd introduce me as such in the cafeteria and the table would relax and people grinned. It was a better ice breaker than "How are we today?" I was very conscious of my voice, I hardly spoke the whole semester, just looked at girls from afar when I drank the Marine's beer.

My next room-mate was a Navy man. Slept with his arms straight down his sides. Never moved. His name was

Delbert and he was tense, tight and never relaxed. He was pasty, had round shoulders, a weak chin and a moustache.

I was a bad influence on him; his grades were fine until he met me. He never drank beer, never smoked and didn't call me anything. At the end of the semester, he dropped out because he said I woke up so late he began to wake up late too. It is an example of How To Influence People by Getting Up Late. If I were Native American, would I be called "He who gets up late" or "He who sleeps in"?

My student adviser was also a Marine and he took me to Veterans House on Locust Lane. He was a dead ringer for John Landis. He said don't look at anybody, don't ask questions and keep your head down. Don't stare and for God's sake, don't smile. He said the Veterans House is where you can get the cheapest beer in State College and shoot pool for free. Thirty-five cents a beer and a dollar coupon will get you three.

Nobody spoke during pool. Nobody laughed and nobody got into a fight. In that solemn atmosphere, you learned to shoot pool well. There was only men in wheelchairs and silent stares, tattoos and facial hair, there were no other students. Nobody ever bothered me in the Veterans House.

I met Rich at a costume party. Halloween. It was in the basement of a frat house, Alpha Chi Ro. He was wearing a mask of Richard Nixon and I was Ronald Reagan with a Catholic collar and a polyester robe down to my ankles. Polyester and rubber is murder. Rich wore a light grey suit nipped at the waist and a blue shirt and tie. Our rubber masks forced us to drink grain punch through straws. He saw me and did the "I am not a crook" deal. He said he liked my costume and I said I liked his suit. He said should we get rid of the masks and I said thank God.

We went outside and smoked a joint. The night chilled my face and my hair was soaked. He told me I had guts to wear Reagan and I said I thought nobody would mind at a party. Rich was the latest in a long line of Republicans in his family. He was the debate champion of Maryland in high school.

Grain punch is one thing, but a joint after sweating 20 pounds and not having smoked for months is another thing entirely. I don't remember saying goodbye to him. I remember cold sweat and somebody putting my legs up on a chair. "Take it easy, Marco." I pulled up the robe, spread my legs and puked between them. Naturally, there was collateral damage. Fortunately, I was in a dark, damp corner away from the throng. Where you puke is important. I don't know what happened to my mask, but a Catholic priest managed to stagger home alone that night. With vomit on the inside of my thighs and a new friend.

There are only two men whose last names I remember from my time at Penn State. One was John Jay Patterson and the other Tom Curd.

Tom and I decided to take the Greyhound to Tempe, Arizona for the game. Penn State had lost the year before to Oklahoma at the Orange Bowl and though we were seven points underdog to the Miami Hurricanes we figured we couldn't let this chance pass. I had missed the Orange

Bowl because I was in London to see my two-timing whore of a girlfriend and my mother. This time Sisyphus was rolling his rock up that mountain again and I wasn't going to miss it, not for all the beautiful women in the world.

We split everything down the middle - the tickets, motel room and booze. We had two-and-a- half bottles each for the two-and-a-half day journey. It meant spending New Year's Eve on the bus. We sat at the back, near the toilet, so we could smoke. Tom suggested we smoke a joint while everybody was sleeping. I pointed out that the bus driver never slept.

Tom was responsible for the more hair-raising ideas on our pilgrimage to Sun Devil stadium, home of Arizona State, an example being the game itself, when the idea occurred to him to piss where we were sitting, surrounded by Miami's faithful.

"Cover me, Marco, it'll only take a minute."

"Can't you hold it in, man?"

"No, I can't."

"Just go to the bathroom. I'll hold your seat."

"No, can't make it, I have to. Cover me, nobody will see."

A girl behind us told her boyfriend and he started yelling. Trust a girl not to be watching the game. The honour of Penn State was compromised, so we had to find some place else to sit.

Tom Curd was six four and large enough for a lineman in high school. When he spoke, it was with extreme deliberation, helmets being what they were in the eighties.

He once thought of trying out for tight end, until he saw what practice was like under Joe Paterno.

Black men in shower caps dotted the bus. The smell of the toilet got to us when we finished the booze. We kept looking for beer, but the bus only stopped at McDonald's. Ohio and Oklahoma flew by. Texas took forever. Pheonix glittered like a giant airport for aliens. The motel was in Mesa and we found an expatriate Penn State bar nearby. We were low on cash, but still had enough for a couple of beers, and Tom was getting on my nerves. We smoked the last of the weed, but that did not solve our cabin fever.

I snapped when I woke up in the morning and Tom had his legs and arms around me, like I was a bolster. "I was only doing it to keep warm, Marco." I yelled at him and he yelled at me.

We were out of booze and dope and we needed cash for the cab. I put it down to lack of alcohol and tension at the prospect of the game. I knew Tom wasn't gay. I was more upset to think he might have thought I was. At least he didn't have a hard on. That would have been an impossible situation. This is why camping is not what I would call a vacation. A bunch of men in a tent.

The sight of the stadium made us friends again; the sight of that bowl rising up like the Taj Mahal on a vast plain in front of a flat-lined horizon, a monument in a sea of sand and tarmac. And seeing other Penn Staters, in navy blue and white, with their banners and round bellies and beers cans. We both pissed over a sandy ledge, a drop in the desert, and I took pictures in black and white.

Sun Devil stadium had a capacity of 72,000, and it was packed. We found two seats in Miami's end-zone. The Nittany Lions never came near it. At one point, the 'Canes had 200-plus total yards, and we had 20. We were right behind the goalposts, but because we were so low, we couldn't see anything up-field.

Tom was restless; the pissing humiliation played on his mind. "Marco, I can't see anything. Why don't we move and see if we can get closer to the fifty-yard line? We can't see anything here Marco." This was midway through the second quarter, I was relieved we had found seats and that the Nittany Lions were still in it. "Marco, let's go over there, over to the twenty-yard line."

"Tom, we already moved once. I'm not going to move again. This is fine."

"But you can't see anything."

He was right, we couldn't see jack, but I was still pissed off at the pissing incident. I told him that if we moved, we would lose.

"Fuck it, Marko, halftime, I'm going."

"Fine. I'm staying here." It took us a while to get these seats, now he is suggesting going right around the end-zone, with ushers, gates, security, and stepping over people and walls. I wasn't going to risk it. This wasn't Asia; you couldn't bloody well sit on the steps.

Besides, I was used to it, not seeing half the game, I mean. What do you think it was like sitting in the freshman/sophomore section at Beaver Stadium? Even when I was a junior, I still sat there, we all did. It was fun, there were marshmallows. People stood up when the wave arrived. People started the wave from that section. "Please do not throw marshmallows at each other as this may cause serious eye injuries," the stadium PA announcer reminded us every game. The trick was to bonk a good-looking girl on the back of the head. It would rain marshmallows for about ten minutes, then everybody ran out. Our 44 oz cups would last till halftime; nobody got kicked out because of marshmallows but plenty were kicked out for alcohol. Smuggling was a serious business, but stewards and keepers of the gate were not going to open every two-litre bottle of Mountain Dew or Coke. The thing was to mix it up, let the foreigner carry the bag.

One game, I forget which, we were up thirty-five to nothing at the half. The wind chill factor drove everyone to seek shelter, to head for home. Our section was cleaned out, except for John Jay Patterson, Tom Curd and yours truly. We still had rum and by God we were going to stick till the end. Tom was waving his giant arms, lost his balance and took John and I down with him, sliding down about eight rows of benches. I must take credit for not exaggerating, because it has been twenty plus years and I could have added a few more rows to our fall, so I hope you appreciate my fealty to the past. Only one player had a chant all to himself - D.J. Dozier; throw both arms up, sway side to side slowly and yell, "Deee Jay, Deee Jay, Deee Jay." Looking at beautiful girls walking up and down the steps, turning round and waving at boys who were not us. Owners of cars being summoned every so often, "Will the owner of … please report to the nearest steward. Will the owner of …"

I was incorrect when I said I remembered only two last names from my time at Penn State. There were the Mullen brothers, Bill and Dave, with whom I shared an apartment for a year, and Scott Gross, my first non-military roommate in the dorms in East Halls.

Bill Mullen was the older brother. He was skinny, had a moustache and would sooner cut his arm off than smoke grass. He came from a part of Pennsylvania that said 'wooter' for 'water'. He was a student, but was a townie surrounded by students. He had a car, and wasn't interested in frat parties, hay rides, St.Patrick's Day, concerts or whatever it was students did. You could tell he was embarrassed to be surrounded by kids. His friends were married and lived in houses of their own.

One weekend he asked if I wanted to go to a party at his friends' place, a couple he'd known from high school. "It's an older crowd, Marko, so don't say anything, don't stare, don't laugh and don't ask any dumb questions. There'll be plenty of beer and a pool table in the basement. It's a really cool house and they're a great couple."

"Will there be any vodka or bourbon?"

"We'll see, Marco. I'll try to get you upstairs if I can."

Bill always chuckled when he introduced me to anybody, whether it was friends or the police.

"This is Marco, he's from Malaysia." He never grew tired of it.

He left me in the basement to join the hosts upstairs. Said he'd be down in a minute. I was hoping it'd be an hour or two. I shot pool with a black man wearing a green hat, sun glasses, jewellery and a tight beige suit. He looked like a coke dealer.

I kept looking at the stairs and wondering; I thought I smelled grass. I thought of going up that stairs, but experience had taught me well. I drank as many beers as I could, and lay down on the sofa.

Bill came downstairs eventually. "Everything alright, Marco? Sorry, man, they don't have enough to go around."

We left the next morning. Coke is for rich people anyway, so I didn't mind.

Dave Mullen was a guitarist. He had a black Fender Strat with a cream fret-board. It was a beautiful guitar, and he put great store in it. He practiced all the time without an amp. His heroes were Yngvie Malmsteen and Eddie Van Halen. Joe Satriani was a given. Randy Rhoads was great, but Jimmy Page and Eric Clapton were overrated dinosaurs with poor technnique. There was no arguing with him. He would tear down all our favourite bands because the lead guitarists weren't good enough. My friends hated him.

I liked him because we could argue for hours, and he'd get into specifics and mimic our guitar gods. We had huge arguments about substance and form, but you couldn't argue with speed and technique and soul was in the ear of the beholder. But we agreed about Roxy Music. And that was enough. "I didn't know who they were, never heard of them, so I didn't wanna go, but my buddy had tickets and he kept asking me, so at the last minute I went. I thought it was gonna be shit, I really did. I swear to God, Marco, they had 15 musicians on stage, and the sound, man, it was perfect, you could hear every one of them, brilliant musicians. It was one of the best concerts I'd ever been to in my life, I swear to God, Marco."

When I ran onto the field after the game ended, I did not recognize anybody. I was looking for Tom. I threw up on the field. This was the second time I had thrown up on the field after a game. The first was at Beaver Stadium when Penn State beat Alabama when both teams were 4-0. The students climbed the goalpost but didn't bring it down. After I threw up on the hallowed surface of Sun Devil Stadium, I felt better. I took photographs, first of the scoreboard which displayed Penn State 14 Miami 10. Then of the field full of blue and white lunatics running in circles and screaming.

Then I saw Scott Gross. "Hey, Feroz." (He knew me before my name was Marco.) We jumped and hugged and jumped and hugged and then he flew away. He was in his uniform, a dark blue suit with a white bib down the front and the letters PSU.

One day he told me he was trying out for the band. He played the trombone.

"The marching band?"

"The band, yeah. I don't know if I'll get in, though."

"Of course you'll get in, you've got the experience."

"We get to go with the team for all the games and stay in hotels and everything."

"Scott, that's fantastic."

"I don't know if I'll get in, though. Practice is six hours a day, and we have to learn to march, and the steps and the music and they yell at you. It's tough."

He was a good kid. He was my roomate before Delbert. Short. Never smoked, drank or cussed; never hassled me at all in our semester together; never practiced in the room and because he was gone the whole day, I had the room to myself, it was like living alone, and when he came back, he was always in a good mood. If he were a girl, I would have married him.

He told me he had made the band. I forced a beer on him and asked if he could get tickets for away games. I had the room to myself on weekends when he went away with the team. That was the year we went 11-0 and lost to Oklahoma in the Orange Bowl.

When Tom had left at half-time for a better view, climbing over railings and avoiding stewards, I had to decide whether to take a piss or not. I would have lost the seat and might have had to stand at the back of the section. I held it in. My kidneys didn't suffer permanent damage when I pissed in my jeans more than two hours later.

A guy, skinny, unshaven, a thin moustache, sat down next to me with a 44 ounce cup, a straw and a drink that was green. Dark green. It was the fourth quarter. We were nervous. Penn State was defending a lead, and it was our end zone.

He offered me his drink. It was vodka and God knows what, but it was strong. Miami was driving down the field. I took tiny sips because the stuff was awful and I didn't want to insult his hospitality.

Then they were on our nine-yard line. We could hear Testaverde yelling. He wanted to pass; we knew it, every down was a pass. We could smell it. Sack! Nine yards loss. Third and goal from the eighteen. Six seconds left. Six.

He dropped back; it was in the air. I saw two guys in line of the flight. Both Blue and White. The first guy caught it. He went down with it. To our right, a seam burst onto the field. The guy with the drink ran down the steps. I stayed where I was because there was one more play. We could still fumble. The invasion was repulsed. They were rounded up and herded off the field. The banks were about to burst. I wondered if I could jump the wall. I prayed for the snap. We took the knee. Game Over. The wall was easy, the drop was a shock. Knees bent and roll over. The field was ours. The night was ours. The country was ours.

I was close enough to photograph Ahmad Rashad and Joe Paterno. They were standing on a platform; our hero Shane Conlan was drowned by heads, shoulders and arms. Years later when I finally saw a recording, a dvd sent by a friend, when Ahmad Rashad said, "Coach, you are the National Champions," and Paterno said, "I think so," my heart swelled and I choked on a sob. I've felt that way a handful of times in my life and it never had anything to do with family, work, women, religion or politics.

"Marco!" I turned around and Tom was bounding toward me like a grizzly at top speed. "We did it! We did it!"

Outside the stadium, the Mecca of our dreams, the Holy Grail of our faith found and reclaimed with six seconds left; clasped to our hearts and infused into our blood streams forever, we waited for a cab and my bladder gave out. By the time I pulled it out, my jeans were soaked and steaming in the January night.

We shared the cab with two students from Miami and they did all the talking. We were squished by irate Miami Hurricane fans who had not conceived defeat. I was worried the cabbie would notice the smell and kick me out.

"I can't believe it, five fucking interceptions."

"Why didn't we run? All we had to do was run it in."

"Testaverde, man."

"He had four fucking interceptions, and he still wanted to pass."

"And we ran thirty-three yards two or three plays before?"

"We ran that whole drive man, that's how we fucking got there."

"What was Johnson thinking?"

"That was Vinny, man."

"Fucking asshole, we threw it away. We had it, Penn State was shit, we gave it away, five interceptions."

"We would have crushed them."

"Easy."

"Four plays and he had to pass on every down."

"Vinny."

"I can't fucking believe it."

"We shoulda just given it to Alonzo."

"They couldn't stop the run, there was no way."

"First and goal ..."

"And Johnson lets Vinny pass."

"Five fucking interceptions."

"Yeah, fucking Vinny, man."

"Did he want to run it in himself?"

"No."

"What was Johnson doing?"

"Nothing."

"First and goal from the nine, and we passed. We gave it to them. They didn't deserve it. We gave it to them."

Tom Curd and I did not speak. We did not have to.

The two-and-a-half days back to State College we had no money and no booze, but we were sleeping easy.

Tomo carried the keg. Jeffro and I hauled the cases. "Here comes the keg," roared Tomo. Jeffro and Dalene kissed.

I looked at Sabine. I was in love with her, but she was going out with Ray because he had spent time in Germany whilst in the army and spoke the language. I was too slow, too scared. Sabine was Dutch, but she knew German.

"Don't come into my kitchen, Marco, I'm making spaghetti" said Dalene.

"And I'm drinking wine," said Sabine.

"We're drinking wine, and you can't have any, Marco."

Sabine's ruby red lips were redder than usual, it was unfair.

"Is Rich coming over?"

"He's on the way. He's picking up Tracy," said John Jay Patterson. He wasn't fond of Tracy. She was a freshman and an airhead.

"Hey Marco, wanna have a hit?"

John and I were not the kind to have one bong hit. We

were the three, maybe four, bong hits type; a one bong hit was just a figure of speech.

"We got your case of ponies."

"It'll wait till game time."

"I don't see what he sees in Tracy," said John.

"How did he meet a freshman? She's too dumb for him," I said.

"It's a cover-up, a smoke screen," John wore an evil grin, "He's gay. He's pretending to be bi."

"He's not gay."

"I know him, Marco, you don't."

"He does overdo the 'I love her tits' stuff."

"You know it, Marco. He's bi, maybe, but definitely more gay than bi."

It's true that Rich always wore his long-sleeved shirts down to his wrists. Why didn't he roll them up? Maybe it was because he was the former debating champion of Maryland and he always had to be formal.

"Well, he is getting laid," I said.

"Yeah."

"Fuck it."

"Yeah."

"Is it my turn?"

"Fuck, yeah."

Bubble, bubble.

"So can we win?"

"I don't know. They're at home. Our offense sucks, except for D.J."

We never jinxed the team. Being nervous suited us. Our offense was never good enough and we always wondered when our luck would run out.

We adjourned to the living room, grabbed our beers. The door flung open and there was Rich with Tracy.

"Hi," Rich said.

"Dude," said John.

"Hi, Tracy," I said.

"Hi."

"Hi Tracy", said Dalene and Sabine from the kitchen.

"Marco, I believe ... shall we?" said Rich. "Tracy darling, excuse us. John, Marco and I have to ..." He kissed her.

She smiled. "Ok." She found space on the sofa. Rich was lucky to have her, she was unshakeable. Nothing bothered her.

I lit the bowl. His finger lifted off the carburetor. He had decent lung power. Maybe because he didn't drink so much. "That girl ... I haven't smoked in days. She's exhausting."

"Another one, Rich?" asked John.

"Please."

A longer hit; no smoke left behind.

"We have enough, scored Thursday."

John took another hit, holding his palm over the bong to finish. My lung power was shot. I had to pass it to Rich to finish. Rich wasn't buying anymore. It happens.

"You picked up the keg?"

"Yeah, it was freezing. Tomo got me up."

"It's good stuff, Marco."

"Dalene's contact. Not many seeds."

"This is better than average, Marco. Let's go again, John, after you."

"Thank you, Rich."

"You're welcome, John."

"Oh, shut the fuck up."

John was a Democrat and Rich a Republican. The three of us talked politics and history on occasion, but never while we smoked. John knew Mondale and Dukakis were useless, Rich knew Reagan was a doddering old fool, especially in his second term. They saw no point defending either side; they were aware of each party's limitations, and Carter was the meeting point of failure. They grew up in Democratic and Republican families; it was hereditary. There was no point in changing the world, especially when the whole world revolved around South Africa. Free Nelson Mandela. Divest in South Africa. Forget about America, that ended in '68, and only a raving lunatic would defend Nixon or Ford or Carter. "We're a consumer society, no longer a manufacturing society," John said.

It was a basement apartment. The view in all three rooms was the bottom of parked cars. You could open the window when there were no cars touching your nose. The address was 228, South Garner Street, apartment 11, State College, PA 16801.

In my first year, nobody else smoked grass, so I spent a considerable amount of time in the bathroom. It was very clean. There was the Pattee library and Burger King if I did not like what was on TV. We drank in the apartment, but I went to bars alone, or to frats with friends. There was a frat party every night, but I wasn't a girl, so it wasn't a daily occupation. In the second year I graduated to the single room as I was the only occupant left. As president of the apartment, I decreed that one could smoke anything anywhere, but many preferred the privacy of my room when thoughts were private. They could come in even when I was sleeping. As long as they woke me up for a hit. It's good to be president.

Dalene and Sabine usually ignored Tracy and other women our circle brought into our lives. They were the first, they were the centre of attraction and they were the only ones our circle cared about. Dalene ran the ship and Sabine sank my boat. Other women were not worth the effort. They had each other and that was enough. Other women were temporary and useless.

Tomo introduced us one night and the four of us shared a bottle of J and B and Dimple that I had bought duty-free for somebody else. They made machines and tortured me by forcing me to drink huge shots against my will. When they saw tears in my eyes, they felt sorry for me and never tricked me again. Machines are liquor and the mixer separated in a shot glass when the mixer is poured carefully through a handkerchief or a bandana.

Dalene had a tiny waist and a high ass. She always wore a grey hat and large glasses that rested on the tip of her tiny nose and covered half her face. Once I offered 20 bucks for a cloth bracelet she was wearing. It was a Dead bracelet. She took it off and gave it to me. "You can only trade, Marco, not sell or buy." I am wearing it now. Her last name was Perry.

Sabine's last name was Prediger. She had beautiful curly blond hair, like a child's, ruby red lips born for kissing and perfect blue eyes. She knew I was head over heels about her and we would watch movies together. When I came home Sabine wrote to me. I never replied. There was no percentage in it. We would stay in Penn State forever.

John, Rich and I used to donate plasma every week; that is, sell it. We'd go in on a Monday, get ten bucks, then again on Thursday, get fifteen and we'd have twenty five each, the amount for an eighth of an ounce. A quarter was forty. We'd score on Friday and have enough for the weekend and Monday night football. Tom wouldn't go so far, and I don't blame him. Ninety minutes with a needle the size of which would make young children and their mothers faint. First they take your blood, spin it around in a centrifuge, take out the white blood cells, then, for the next forty five minutes put it back. Ninety minutes with a giant needle in our arms just so we could buy grass. My left arm is scarred still, twenty years later. My Penn State tattoo.

"Marco, Dalene wants you to bring the bong out," Sabine said from behind the door.
"Yeah, Marco, come on guys, the game's gonna start," Dalene yelled.
"We'll be right there," John said.
Session over. Time to watch an undefeated Penn State play in white at South Bend, Indiana.
I tried to keep a diary from that summer of '88, but I always thought keeping a diary was for those in love with

themselves. It is different if you are in jail, in solitary. Life has to be lived, and if one forgets, so be it. There are names in the diary that I cannot put a face on. The ones I remember are in my heart.

Dalene and Crazy Bob and Crazy Mike had a place called Heartbreak Hotel, at 220 1/2, South Fraser Street, State College, PA 16801. There was a large basement with wide stairs coming down one side of a horseshoe-shaped floor. There were sofas, posters, home-made flags, rugs, lamps, a bar and on one wall was spray painted "Heartbreak Hotel". There was a fridge and a stereo. Dalene fixed it so that my farewell party would be there. One last blowout to send me home in style.

Dalene was our pied piper. She led us on our merry dance. Like a mama duck with her chicks on a crystal cold lake. One time we ran all over campus and ended up in a tree. Each person had a branch to sit on. We looked like the Brady Bunch.

When we walked into the Civic Arena in Pittsburgh for the Dead we all held hands. We were tripping our heads off at the tailgate. She made sure no one got separated, so no one would freak out. Before we got to our seats, John had an epileptic fit. He fell to the floor and convulsed. We couldn't do anything but make a circle. If the stewards and security saw him, he would have to be taken to a tent, and we might have been kicked out, too. By sheer force of will he made it stop. It lasted about a minute, but we were scared. John looked okay, but it blew our minds and God knows how he felt.

When the lights went down and the music played, he was in familiar territory. When he said he was alright, we were alright. Close call. When you're tripping all you can say is phew.

Before the concert was the tailgate. At the tailgate we sat tt the back of Paul's car with the keg in the open trunk and tie-dyed t-shirts laid out on a white sheet on the ground in front of us. We were trying to sell t-shirts.

It is easy making tie-dyed t-shirts. All you needed was a fork. We did it in the laundry room in the girl's dorm. I wasn't supposed to be there, and I got caught by Ginger, the RA, and, of course, I was drinking. Ginger knew me, but she busted me anyway. Art without sacrifice is nothing.

I lined up for hits of nitrous oxide. It was a dollar and a guy shot a hit into your mouth. I am sure we did not sell a single t-shirt.

In the middle of the first set, when everyone was dancing, Paul freaked out. He sat down with his head in his hands and yelled, over and over, "My keys, my keys, I left my keys in the goddamned car." He was going on and on about his car and how he was going out to check on it. He wanted me to go with him. I said no. Dalene and Sabine dumped water on his head and it worked. Paul freaked out because the trunk of his car was open, there was a keg in it, the doors were open, the keys were in the ignition and Crazy Steve was the only one there. Crazy Steve didn't have a ticket. He wanted to trip. Besides he'd seen the Dead about two dozen times. Paul danced the rest of the concert, even during "Space" and "Drums" when everyone else sat down.

We were still tripping when the concert ended. We had joints which made us trip again. The music haunted us. We talked about the songs. And the scene was re-lived. Oh the segues by the real pied piper, Jerry Garcia. On the way home our two cars were separated, found each other, then lost each other again. At a red light in downtown Pittsburgh we were side by side, screaming and shouting with relief, raising and showing our shabbily constructed joints, so happy to see one another; then the light turned green and we shot off in different directions.

State College did not have an airport. I was flying out of Harrisburg early the next morning. Dalene woke me up last of all, said everything was packed and we were late. Paul was driving, John was shotgun and Dalene, Sabine and I were in the back. Paul said he could try to make it in an hour, but forty-five minutes was unlikely. I did not want too much luggage, so I gave most of my things away. Sabine and Dalene inherited my sweaters and shirts. John gave me a box of Dead bootlegs. Still there was too much weight for that little yellow car.

We rushed to the counter. I had missed my flight by a mile. I made a reservation for the same flight the next morning. John laughed and said we could smoke some more. Another party at the Heartbreak Hotel. Everyone tried his best, but was too burnt out by the night before. Tom said goodbye early. Tomo was already back at home, the same with Jefro.

Again, we were late; Paul gunned his car to the airport, but he was low on water and the engine started to smell. Two long trips in two days were too much for his car. Paul's engine seized at the airport.

Sabine, Dalene and I rushed with my luggage and as I looked behind, Paul's head was in his hands as smoke issued from under the hood. Sabine kissed me for the last time. I hugged Dalene and asked, "How are you going to get back?"

"Never mind that, Marco, don't worry about us, just go."

We won at Notre Dame 21-16 to stay undefeated. The Nittany Lions still haven't won a National Championship since the season of 1986. In a selfish way it makes me feel good, that we were the last batch of students to run onto the field, to know what it was like to win it all. But I think Joe Paterno deserves another and I hope the man gets it. On the goal line with six seconds left.

fireworks

••••

People were standing, not moving, outlines etched in sharp relief by the clear, clean orange light. Murmurs. Everybody murmuring. "He was very dejected, very dejected," a friend said with an exasperated sigh, the eyes pleading, the voice wavering and dying. His friend doesn't look at him. In the background, high above and far away from the house, a tower stands black and unlit. Birds sit on the roof uncannily spaced, symmetrically apart. I thought they were pieces of wood sticking out from the roof. Then one flew off.

The sun was creeping out of view behind the tower, as if to say, "I can't help you, I'd like to but my time is up, you'll have to make do." There are two ladies leaning on Mike's car; one has tissue in hand, and a pathetic, quizzical frown on her face, she is silent but her head bobs slowly from side to side.

No car can pass. We are standing all over the road. Suddenly a shriek, followed by a long low moan. Sunitra's mother grieves for her son. Other voices join in, and soon there is a monotonous, chanted wail.

So many people are standing outside Sunitra's house motionless, powerless, like pigeons, stupidly, silently looking this way and that. The woman leaning on Mike's car feels my stare, turns around, but doesn't see me. She dabs the right eye and murmurs to the woman at her side, who makes no sign, save for a slight nod. They are both old. They've seen a lot of funerals and their looks and gestures are practised to perfection. A man next to them smiles while he relates information that has been passed round and round, uprooted, churned out, dug up and regurgitated, from early that morning when they first heard about it, to when the body comes back from the airport, and probably still when his coffin goes up in flames and it will continue on tomorrow and the day after, day and night, unceasing, relentless, unstoppable, for the next 45 days, which is the decent minimum specified for mourning, expected by society, with prayers every day in the evenings. Every day for 45 days.

And probably after.

The light on white walls was pale amber. Faces looked more thoughtful, pensive, dignified. The strong black of sunless, sheltered spaces softened to damp, deep blue. The sky on my right was pursuing lilac.

And still the people stood, and still we blocked the road. Waiting for the body, waiting for showtime. A Japanese man comes through the crowd. Yvonne turns to us, "That's his boss, I think," she whispered, "he worked in Singapore. Japanese boss." He is quite young, with hair touching collar; he wears a dark blue suit and strides into the house towards the wailing throng. A fair Indian woman blows her nose; the birds have left the rooftop; the bottom of light grey clouds is painted softly red.

The Japanese man comes out, talks to someone, hesitates, then is off. Back to Singapore; to the office where he is boss, where Sunitra's brother used to work. For him, it is a death in the office; for others, that of a friend, for others still, death of all hope and meaning.

And still the people stand; the body is not back yet. "Sunitra has gone to the airport to pick up her brother," said Jessie, a friend, "you're still in shock, I see," for I made no sound. "Bullshit," thought I, "wrong again. So much for bloody woman's intuition." "Selamat Hari Raya, huh?" she continued. I replied, "Hmmph," which I do often, for it seems to says a lot and is usually, though not often enough, fatal to unwanted and unnecessary conversation. "Yeah, yeah," I thought, "It happens on holidays too," as I remembered a certain Christmas and a certain coffin. She always sounds so earnest and definite but unfortunately her speech reverberates with twangs of Strine, on account of living in Brisbane. She is tall and graceful and has beautiful brown eyes. She is the kind of woman I would gladly kiss to make her shut up.

The neighbours, a Chinese family, crane their necks and look like beakless penguins staring over the red brick wall. The mother of the family is cradling a young child; she grips him fast. He is curious and apprehensive, struggling, wriggling, trying to get free. She holds him tighter and then bounces him in her arms.

The hearse arrives, carrying Sunitra and her dead brother's body.

A few days later, it was April Fool's day.

A firework exploded, and another. A car horn at some distance beeped twice; then another bangclap. Silence.

The air-conditioner hums, softly halting, humming, apologetically endless. Ten little tablets. "What was that?" "Sunitra tried to commit suicide last night," the voice on the telephone said. "Commit suicide?" I said. "My foot," I thought. No, no, that wasn't "trying to commit suicide". No sir, she tried to kill herself maybe, but commit suicide? No, not classy enough, not clever or serious or gutsy enough. Plain fucking stupid. Swallowing ten pills. "Ooooohhh, I want to leave this world, I want to die and go to him! I want to join my breder! I want to be with my breder!"

Fucking weak, selfish, thoughtless.

Later, she told me that when she left for the airport to retrieve her brother's remains, one of her cousins, who was with her in the hearse, said, "Hey, Sunitra, you got the car number, ah? Your brother's car number, do you know it? Huh? Sunitra, hey, the number, girl, the number."

When the all-white hearse arrived, she was sitting in front, wearing big, aviator sunglasses and as soon as the van stopped, she flew to her father, her voice raised and garbled. She said something over and over again to her father, hugging him, holding tight. When the coffin was slowly dragged out of the back of the hearse, the father let out a soft sob and cried. Sunitra rended the air with a crumbling, shattering cry, repeating over and over again a chant, a phrase, a prayer.

Because of the way he died, the coffin was closed. "Let me see my son, I want to see my son," screamed the mother, each time louder and more resolute, supported and held at each arm by friends of the son, "Auntie please, auntie, please auntie, don't, don't auntie, you cannot auntie, please understand, please calm down, please auntie." "My son! I want to see my son, he's my only ...." But the coffin was closed and not to be opened.

"He was her only son. He looked out for her and he was angry with me and my father for being dismissive of and indifferent to her," said Sunitra before she took pills the next day.

After her son's death, Sunitra's mother's state of mind was such that she accused Sunitra of the most heinous crime, of casing the greatest wrong, of being responsible for her own brother's death. Sunitra's crime was in bringing bad luck to the family. She'd always been bad luck, she was told. God was punishing them for Sunitra's sins. She was always a bad girl. She never listened. She wasn't married. No one wanted her, she wasn't good, no, she wasn't like her brother.

Sunitra listened in stupefaction. What was there to say in reply? To think ... And what do you know, here comes auntie and grandma, sister and mother, sarees trailing, eyes narrowing, hissing between their teeth, "Yes, yes, she was always a bad girl, she never listened to her poor, dear mother, she always thought she knew everything, showing off, being clever, answering back, always answering back, she caused her poor, dear mother so much pain, that girl."

And still they continued, every day they were there at Sunitra's house and every day they talked and talked, with stern and sour faces, all the while completely ignoring Sunitra's mother who, at this time, was given to pacing around the house, talking aloud to walls and pictures and herself; Grandma imparting pearls of wisdom, "Look at her, look at her hair. I never see her in a saree and she acts as though there's nothing wrong with her, at this age (25) and still not married, not even engaged. She's very dark, not fair at all like her mother, not fair like us, you can see why she's not married, of course, no one wants her."

When Sunitra's mother snapped out of her reverie, she would start on Sunitra again, and auntie and grandmother would reload and fire point blank shots at Sunitra's face; revelling in her abject misery as they did so.

She could not put up with it any longer, her father, her only hope, was not equipped to deal with the knives, barbs and venom of the three women. Indeed, he was not even inclined to stop them. He was not inclined to do anything at all; and so she felt the situation hopeless, she really truly absolutely thought the situation hopeless.

The family doctor was livid. "They are not supposed to give out more than eight pills, how could they give her ten pills? Even eight is too many, for heaven's sake, eight pills are lethal! What was that doctor thinking? A doctor like him should be reported and dealt with, harshly dealt with, oh dear, oh dear, oh dear."

I don't think they ever got round to busting him or suing him, it was just talk for the moment, performance for the day, hot air from the weak middle-aged to belong to the circle of sorrow wrung dry. For 45 days, everybody and his mother would have a shot.

A lightning flash, it's going to rain, the sky shows itself to be mother of pearl and dark blue at the sides, and then darker still opposite the setting sun. An Indian man with a prodigious, if predictable, paunch steps forth and begins to direct the proceedings. Several rings of flowers are thrust into the hearse. These are yellow, white, pink, peach, salmon and they stand on rickety, fragile, cane legs. The driver of the hearse puts the flowers in with not a trace of solemnity, much less reverence, he is doing his job, and would like to be on his way. A wreath of flowers gets caught in the door that he has shut impatiently. It sticks out of the white van/hearse choking, entangled, hideously strangled. No one thinks to put the wreath in and shut the door proper and tight. All of us stand there and ignore it, leaning now on one leg, now on the other, some with gaping mouths, some digging noses.

Sunitra wants to ride in front. She wants to go in the hearse, she wants to go with her brother. For some reason, they won't let her, too many already. "Please girl, go with uncle, he'll take you there, he'll take you there, you'll be right behind us, go in the car girl, please girl, it's all right you'll be right be ... OK, OK, put her in the back, you can go in the back, OK girl? You go in the back, there, there, that's all right, now that's all right, you'll be with your brother." So she sat there amidst the flowers, holding on tight to the coffin.

It starts to drizzle: because of the rain, people sway and shift, things are acting up, the body is going soon, time to get ready, time to hitch rides, "Are you going?", "No priests are coming because it's an unnatural death. They won't come," said Jessie. Unnatural death? A car crash? For this, priests make themselves scarce? "Spare me ...", "No, it's true," said Jessie, "the parents have to do everything themselves. Do you suppose the crematorium is open?", "Of course it's open .... Isn't it?"

No, no, she was wrong again, that stupid ..., I don't know why I get so worked up, listening to these people; she wasn't wrong about the priests, though.

The rain splashed onto the road splintering, shattering into brilliant points and circles of light, mocking. People were beginning to go. I had decided not to. Mike was going, because he knew the guy, then again maybe he didn't. None of us, Kelvin, Sunny, Yvonne nor I ever met Sunitra's brother. We were there because she was our friend, and at funerals they never refuse anyone admittance, everyone is invited. Unlike weddings. Labels, strings, ties, they mean little or less than usual at death's appearance. Family ties, what an abominable lie in most cases. They've known us from the day we were born, but remain resolute, complete, total, absolute and utter strangers. Oblivious, indifferent, exhausted.

Thank God for friends.

Else I would have gladly died long ago.

Kelvin and Yvonne didn't want to go to the cremation either. Sunny, dependable and right and loyal as ever, thought he should go, at least to save Mike the experience of having to go alone; he would go with Mike.

I walked down the road to Kelvin's car. Kelvin and Yvonne were ahead of me, hurriedly trying to get out of the strengthening rain. After I had walked ten or so steps I turned back. I would go also.

When I got to Mike's car, Mike was ready to go but Sunny was missing. We waited for Sunny; then these Singaporeans came hurtling into our car, "Can you give us a lift, can you, there are three of us, are you going? Can you give us, you're going aren't you? Can you please, three of us, give us a lift? Can you, could you, hello."

We said, "N, no. I'm sorry, we're waiting for someone, there's someone else coming, our friend, waiting for our friend, sorry, no." Then we said, "OK, I guess, yeah we could take, we could yeah, could take, I guess we could take two of you, could take two of you, but only two, there's someone else, yeah OK."

Then Sunny came running, "I go in Kelvin's car, la, we follow you," while the rain poured around him and the black turbulent sky paralysed all with the sound of chilling, hostile thunder. "OK, you sure, ah?" I said as he ran away through the crisscrossing and disappearing headlights.

The Singaporeans erupted. "Aaah, we can take three, we can take three, we can take, Kenneth, Kenneth, Ken, Ken, HERE, over here, heyey, KEN, this car, this car, come on." The car door is pushed out, a wet body thumps into the back seat, bringing with it a stinging breeze, the door thuds shut and there are three Singaporeans sitting in the back seat.

The whole way, they didn't even bother to fucking introduce themselves. They might have mumbled thanks for something or other. Mike and I remained silent, we were not exactly chatty, we listened to the music through his blown-out speakers, as the Singaporeans whispered amongst each other, carrying themselves and their world with them wherever they go.

We made it to the crematorium but Sunny, Kelvin and Yvonne didn't. In the rain and the glare they followed the wrong car and got lost.

I was surprised when they set fire to the coffin. I hadn't expected it. When we got there the coffin was in place. The enclosure was long and high, with white surfaces long since etched by grey, open to the elements, supported by pillars, surrounded by a low, thick concrete wall; rounded and softened by the desperate, fevered, unconscious, cold hands of mourners through the years. It was still raining - it wasn't raining, it was roaring. The coffin was placed on dark, wooden logs, several of them, larger ones below, smaller and shorter ones on top. As before, all the people remained standing, this time all eyes facing the coffin, the men of the family around the father, a handful of friends around Sunitra. Her mother had not come, or rather, she was in no position to attend, perhaps she was advised not to, in any case, she was left behind, sedated by a doctor more than likely.

The priest was responsible for starting things: first this, then that, then the other. Nothing could be heard save the crashing rain and amidst the standing people and the cold, hurrying wind and the bent over, sobbing human that was Sunitra, that man began to sing. He sang alone and quickly, The song sounded old, very old, and sad and weary. The voice sliced through the rain, not booming nor low nor ominous and neither shrill nor persistent, nor damning. Just higher than usual, rising, falling, quavering, patient, matter of fact, irrevocable.

And then the rice. A mound of rice grain, uncooked, was heaped upon a large, flat, tin dish. It was placed at the side of the coffin, next to the head, with the priest standing next to it. You had to climb three steps up to the coffin where the dish and the priest were, to release a handful of grains of rice on the coffin. For some reason, when they began to implore people to go up the steps, to start it off, as it were, most were slow to react and I found myself the third person in line to sprinkle rice onto his coffin. I had never met Sunitra's brother, didn't even know what he looked like.

Slowly a queue formed, waddling, swaying forward with more and more coming out from the shadows, treading lightly over steps, eyes glancing all over. Cupped hands cradling rice, would slowly pull apart while moving in a slow arc over the coffin.

She had to be led there, the last to go. No need to describe her face, suffice to say, grief. She raised her cupped hands over her head, speaking to the gods, before releasing the rice, and she took another handful, caressing her brother's coffin this time, and she took another and another until there was nothing left. She did not want to go, she had to be led down slowly but forcefully by the silent and understanding priest.

Large, yellow slabs of ghee, the length of a large loaf of bread, were heaped onto and around the coffin. They torched it from all sides. As the ghee melted and burned, it left shiny, silvery streaks crisscrossing the top and sides of the coffin. It slid and dropped onto the logs, shrinking, reducing, disappearing. Thus the sound of the crashing rain was overcome and swallowed whole by the crackling flames which threw themselves up, high, towards the roof of the enclosure, not reaching it but seemingly determined to lick and catch something, anything, so that it might not burn alone.

It was not the thing to do to hang around until the fire died out. I would've liked to, but the crowd of friends, co-workers, family and perhaps one or two lovers slipped away, having their last look, stare, glance at the chanting whispers of the ever-circling, eradicating, annihilating flames. The coffin was bright red from the yellow glare, black edges trimming the evanescent, transitory flames, thick grey smoke climbing the eaves, set free into the wet, the dark, the rain. The light danced on the pillars and floors and on faces, but it was over, it was done.

Sunitra was surrounded and led away, through the corridor, through the wide concrete circle. Stopping, turning around, slowing down, turning around, stopping again for another look, another look, and yet another, being pulled gently away, whispered words.

I stopped and turned around, for my last look. The flames must have been nine feet tall, at least.

"Let me see," she screamed, "he's my brother, why won't you ... I must. ..." She was at the car, the car door was opened, she said his name over and over, she said goodbye, was gently pushed in and the car door slammed.

I asked Mike what he thought about waiting for the Singaporeans. "Fuck 'em," replied Mike. So we climbed into his dark grey Mazda 323 with the shitty sound system, and drove away, and all of a sudden, I saw my own funeral in my mind.

Surrounded by a language I do not understand (Arabic), on account of learning the Quran parrotlike when young. Surrounded by people I do not know and will never comprehend (my relatives). And I thought of my friends who would not be able to read an eulogy for me, much less act as pall bearers for me, as I had being, once, for my father.

As that thought seared through my head, I unfastened the seat belt, wound down the window, the wind in my ears as I pushed my head out. And I screamed.

An early version of 'Fireworks' was published in SKOOB Pacifica Anthology No. 2, 1994.

ladder in the water

••••

They were protected by clouds. The orange slanted light flung out by the sun softened and dispersed to embrace, warm, and lightly tint the bodies of the men and women who were on the beach that day, that day that seemed to erupt with optimism, tangible and expected, brushing people's faces with a breeze. New Year's Eve, 1993.

The waiters glided with silent smiles amidst murmurs of approbation and tenderness uttered by people sitting at their lacquered wooden tables, comfortable and calm in their indulgence, sedate and peaceful in their enjoyment, heavy silences between mundane questions and answers pregnant with memories and resolutions. A man, 100 feet above, knotted and held up by a bag of air, dragged by a line soaring from a frenetic, bouncing speedboat, flew past looking at them.

At a table sat a white couple, heavy-set with blotchy skin. The rich orange haze slid through the leaves and branches of awkward, angular trees to smack the profile of the man and the head and shoulders of the woman with a sharp, brilliant light that was temporarily trapped in the man's forearm and the woman's curly, copious blond hair. The curve of a woman's back passes into view, straightening and relaxing with every alternate step; her chin and eyes steady in a graceful aquiline profile, never wavering, unsmiling. She wears a dark two-piece under her thin cotton shirt, open in front, exposing her firm thighs straddled across a speckled grey horse, her skin a glistening shade between tea and honey.

The crawling, glittering sea heaved before them, hiding deep below the churning, ominous, low roar that builds inexorably to a sudden rush and thump onto the surface before it dissipates, hissing its curses while crawling reluctantly backwards.

Christine sat on the edge of the bed, looking at her hair helixing around her right index finger, her nails the colour of fresh blood, eyes blank. She would gave him five more minutes.

"The only way to keep a relationship alive is to remain silent," she thought, while looking at her hair, "staying silent must be the guilty, cop-out saviour of all relationships. That's an ugly word, 'relationship, to describe all that, an ugly word, like 'hospitalization' and 'insurance'."

It was too late anyway. She only had to speak. Of course, that was the hardest part.

Kit was outside, obstinately holding on to the railing, wouldn't go in, wouldn't speak unless spoken to. He wanted to look at her, but settled for leaning on the railing of the balcony; on the 28th floor of their rented apartment, his back to the tinted French windows which separated Christine and Kit, Kit in the sun, Christine invisible behind the reflection. He was thinking of something to say. But looking down from the balcony to the streets below, he forgot what it was he was supposed to say.

The tinted French windows reflected the bay, with its slip of sea and two low, rounded hills, all trapped in a net of gold, more solid and tangible than real life. He turned around and picked up his glass.

"There's four people in the pool," he said, "three guys and a girl... or maybe it's two guys and two ... I'm not sure."

"Do you want to go?" Christine asked, flat and dead, devoid of interest. She forgot the question before she finished it.

"No," Kit said, "there's people there."

She frowned for an instant, hesitant, wary. That tone made it impossible for her; she slid off the edge of the bed and sat cross-legged on the deep blue carpet.

A white spinning sphere languidly completed its arc, caroming off outstretched flailing arms. The ball is civilly retrieved by a middle-aged American lady, sunglasses stuck in front of her flower-print floppy hat. The ball lofts and sits silent in the air before the bashful Malay waitress cuts into sight. "JD Coke?" she inquired, checking; "Gin Tonic and Black Label soda and Vodka Tonic."

"I think we should order a jug next round," declared Kelvin. This was met with general approval. "Ya, cheaper," bleated Yvonne.

Then everyone changed their minds. They would stick with hard liquor; it was New Year's Eve after all.

Nearby, a group of young Japanese men and women were confronting an inflexible gang of five teenaged Indian boys, who were adamant in not wanting to lower the price for 15 minutes on the jet skis. It didn't matter to them that the visitors wanted a package deal, they couldn't care less. Try the banana boat," they said, "it's cheaper," referring to the blue and yellow dinghy that rolls and lurches miserably, apologetically, above the water. But the Japanese wanted to fly, none of that puttering about in a stupid rubber boat; they wanted the jet skis, and so they paid.

Time was when only bodies threw themselves into the water, to dive, splash, make trails which foamed on the surface of the water, ephemeral signatures burning bright silver, sometimes washed with the red of living, breathing life. The sound of roaring cast only by the sea, engulfed within the constant sibilance of the water, accompanied by the sighing, breathing wind.

Now, all that activity was confined to one sorry-looking square; cordoned, fenced in by black plastic rope, supposedly for protection against the hot-dogging, zigzagging, criss-crossing ubiquitous jet skis, not forgetting the skimming darting speedboats blasting and cleaving the air with the drone and whine of their engines.

The magic minute occasioned by a Malaysian sunset threw out as its defiant farewell a red glow edged with salmon, ascending into grey, hovering behind the low black hills, secretive, alluring.

"We have run out of things to toast," declared Kelvin, whilst holding his glass in mid- air. They were frozen in action, while minds remained perplexed..

"Perhaps we could drink to that dog (pronounced dawg) that's running on the beach over there," said David, drawling.

"Why should we drink to that particular dog?" enquired Kelvin.

"Perhaps if he knew us in another lifetime, he would return the compliment." This statement was considered at length by the company.

"I'm afraid that's not a good enough reason to drink," said Kelvin.

"Is there ever a good enough reason to drink?" countered Kamarul.

"Blasphemy!" shouted one and all.

"Another crack like that and you're on the next flight home," said Guru.

"Next boat home, next boat," added Michael.

"Yeah, thanks a lot guys, I'm from Penang, remember?" said Kamal, which is what we usually called Kamarul.

"Well, then we'll send you away, yeah away, awaaayyy, exiled to Shah Alam. Heaven forbid, you'll never see Gurney Drive again."

"Oi, oi, oi," said Kelvin calling the table to order, "What we need now is input of a practical ..."

"... and sensible ..." cut in David.

"Yes, thank you David," continued Kelvin, "nature."

"Not to mention honourable," chimed in Douglas.

"Certainly, no mention, no mention," muttered Kelvin. "So! Any suggestions? And no dogs please."

"That rules out your sister," said David.

Kelvin decided to hit him, then not, then his eyes narrowed and his forefinger waved. "Hey, family, don't play."

"Shall we join the others at the beach?" asked Christine, her voice trailing mid-sentence when she realised he would be irritated and not moved to answer the question.

"Others, always others," thought Kit, "Why can't you sit still with me for once, for New Year's Eve at least, why can't you at least come out to this damn balcony, why can't you just be with me, for once."

Christine got up and flicked away at dust on her jeans. She yawned and headed for the bathroom.

They watched as Yvonne fled in the direction of the bathroom at the back of the garden of the Rasa Sayang Hotel.

"So you gonna get married or what?" asked Kamal.

"No fucking way, lah!" countered Kelvin.

"Better not let her hear you say that," said Mike, grinning, weary and wise.

"Ah, she knows, she doesn't bring it up."

"She will," intoned Seng.

"Bet you Kelvin gets married first," said Guru, looking for trouble.

"Bet you Guru dies first," fired Kelvin.

"Relax Kelvin, it's too early to get violent," said Mike, "even for you, still a long way to go man."

"Yeah, chill, order something, yeah, order something civilised and Guru shut up," added the present company. "Miss, miss, nine tequila shots, please."

"O.K, all ready? Standby salt, lime. The tray has landed."

"I hate tequila," said Douglas.

"We know you do. We enjoy seeing you suffer. We suffer with you, Douglas. O.K, here we go, don't fuck around, salt's melting"

Guru couldn't resist, "Wait, wait, a toast, to Kelvin getting fucked for life, no, I mean it man, I'm happy for you, I'll be your best man."

"That will not happen," answered Kelvin unsteadily, as a broken chorus of gasps and grunts erupted around the table.

"Kelvin, you have our permission to beat the shit out of Guru," said Kamal. "After the next round, of course."

"Amir, why so quiet? Want me to whack you, ah? Drink, man, forget her, it's New Year's Eve lah, forget her."

"It's precisely because its New Year's that he seems so affected," ventured Mike.

"Aahh don't worry, there is a cure, there is hope," added Kelvin.

"Which is?"

"Miss, miss," called Kelvin. David and Douglas began squirming in their chairs in earnest attempts to catch the attention of the fleet-footed and fast disappearing waiters. Finally, one was snagged.

"Long Island, please."

"Can I clear these away?" the waitress said, indicating the glasses.

"I'd rather listen, that's all," said Amir.

"Yeah, you can talk, you're just hung up on that Chinese girl of yours."

"Don't mention her name, man," said Kamal.

"Why?"

"The fucker cannot take it."

"Ooohh."

"Marriage," said Amir, "is the beginning of every single barrier."

"Oh, oh," Kamal was smiling as were the rest.

"Religion," said Amir louder, "faith, race, belief, colour, language, nationality, all are dependent upon the insoluble, institutionalized official outrage, the societal sham, farce, disgrace called marriage."

"He's just pissed off because he tried and cannot dapat this chick," said Kamal.

"Perhaps alcohol should not figure in your short term plans," suggested Douglas.

"Don't worry Amir, we won't bring up the subject again unless somebody brings it up and we all agree that, marriage is a barrier etc, etc."

"What?" asked Yvonne, who had returned from the ladies in time to hear this last exchange.

"We're all sympathizing with Amir who's under tremendous stress, can't you see?" answered Kelvin.

"Oh! Vivi again, ah?" she yelled, "Find somebody else. Move on with your life."

"Hear, hear" said the rest.

"Women never give chance, one," said Seng, who never drank much because he couldn't.

"Thanks for the advice. Can we drop the subject, please?" said Amir.

"At least you won't get married first," said Guru. "I mean, look at Kelvin, he's fucked, man."

"Excuse me," Yvonne said, "he's not fucked, he's happy. You gonna let him talk like that, ah?" she said to Kelvin, her beloved.

"Guru knows I'm gonna whack him soon, within the next half an hour, I'm gonna whack the shit out of him for you, my darling."

"Thank you."

"You're welcome. What about wine?"

"Can, can," said Mike.

"I say we get a bottle of white wine," said Kelvin to change the subject.

Guru was upset. "Wine, you've got to order two bottles, and you won't get that fucked up, but if we order a Tanqueray, you know, a bottle ..."

The chilled Chardonnay from Australia was produced rattling on ice in its wooden bucket.

The light of the dying sun reflected off the metal railings bordering the people-packed terrace, giving it a coat of copper. The trees were dark and silent, though more intimate than ominous; the beach was pockmarked with transient marks for a day almost over in a year almost over.

The bathroom door shut with a click.

Mind reader. Yes, thought Kit, she's a hell of a mind reader. He almost laughed. The breeze felt cool on his face. All we've been through and she can still look at me as if at a stranger. Long ago when I looked into her eyes she looked back at mine, telling me she was not mine, daring me, asking me, but always looking straight back at me. She didn't give a damn what the others thought. I was an ear, a shoulder, a distraction, her different scene. An inconvenient scene, in the end. I shouldn't have fallen so hard for her, but I had no choice; she had won my heart without even trying. "The more women I meet, the better you look," I told her once. She was delighted and said I was crazy. I shouldn't have told her that. I shouldn't have said a lot of things.

She shut the door. He's being so theatrical, she thought. So dramatic, everything's a big scene with him; if he could only see himself, standing there on that balcony, not wanting to come in, waiting for me to do something, if he could only see himself sometimes, he might get his sense of humour back. Probably not. With that thought she set off for the kitchen to scramble some eggs.

Kit heard the fridge door slam. Hard to get. She prefers playing it that way when the odds are in her favour. Something about being Catholic. Probably mandatory to put up a fight. We both knew what would happen next. She, silent, indifferent, waiting for me to force the issue, I playing my assigned part of immoral invader of the virtue of Catholic girls; preparing to receive the unpredictable, sometimes violent, response, and in turn, feeling shocked and outraged after which I would do one of two things; kiss her on the neck at a spot just behind her left ear or drop everything and disentangle myself, moving to the side of my bed (if we were in bed) or if we were up and about, walking away from her, stopping at a suitable distance, face turned steadfastly away from her, obstinately looking down, murderously silent. Then I will feel her face against my back, her breasts, her waist; and her arms would embrace and caress, while from her lips whispered apologies and earnest justification issued. I would capitulate with hidden glee, knowing I had only to turn around, to descend to her lips and bliss.

There was a stiff glass of Jack Daniels and Coke on the balcony table, but he just sat there, not picking up the glass. Kit could hold his liquor, but what had seemed an advantage at times now seemed to him a cruel disadvantage.

He took a sip, and then drained the glass. Warmth slowly coursed through him. He was surprised that it was good, that these moments, which made the balcony bright and sterile, which made the air chill, should exist.

"Hey," said Christine.

"Hey," said Kit quietly.

"It's a holiday. Don't you like holidays?" she added, from the kitchen.

He couldn't suppress a smile. "Yeah, I love holidays, nothing but wonderful memories."

"Uh-huh," she replied.

"Why don't you come out here? What are you doing? Come out here, lah, for a second or something."

"I'm watching T.V. Do you want some scrambled eggs?"

"No thanks."

"O.K," she said as she sat down on the rattan sofa facing the T.V.

He couldn't think of anything to say. They should go down to the beach to join the others, but he didn't feel like going yet, and to his surprise she didn't pursue the matter. But it was still early. He felt like he should sit and not go in until after midnight. The bottle was hardly touched, he could do it easily. If he waited long enough, he might be lucky to hear the front door slam. With only silence to deal with upon coming in from the balcony. With guiltless silence, no acting necessary. Round One won, without spiteful recrimination or delirious cross-examination;

winner by default, but a winner, nonetheless. If only he could hear the front door slam.

The Oprah Winfrey show was on. Christine watched it, somewhat disinterested. Listening to the racket made by the impassioned, sincere figures on T.V., she couldn't rid herself of the thought that Kit would have to be told. She had to tell him she couldn't be with him tonight. He would make a fuss, of course, begging for sympathy in ways like a child demanding attention, by cynically bawling his lungs out, knowing that only with such desperation could success, however temporary, be obtained, feigning vulnerability, making a sodden, sorry spectacle of himself.

A shiver went through Christine. She set the plate on the low wooden table in front of her, because she felt suddenly hollow. She did not want to tell him, it was unthinkable. No sad beauty nor noble grace, only wretchedness and ugliness and all because of a lack of tact, civility and form.

Men and women, earnest, passionate, unflaggingly sincere in their exhortations; pedantic, empty-headed and horrifying decent. They were talking about the need to communicate. A man stood up and told the crowd the story of his life, with a sad, sobering beginning, "I was conceived in sin," he intoned, whilst nodding to let the profundity settle; an awful middle, "My daddy never spoke to me again after that night," and a happy ending. His audience made up of the selfsame sober, sincere and awe-struck, nodded with understanding and reverence and clapped to show their appreciation for this selfless show of sharing.

She shook her head as she got up off the sofa, flicking away unseen dirt, shaking off in her mind life's questions answered before the commercial break.

The deep blue eyes of the three-year-old German girl were fixed upon a spot high up near the top of the huge white colossus all clean, perfect and impressive (at least to a three-year-old) wherein she could see two flecks or spots meandering across a balcony. Her eyes flashed with the knowledge of a tangible fact recorded after which she tugged on her mother's hand and said, "Look mama, people." Then the German girl spotted a cat and forgot about them. Her mother had not looked, in any case.

The wind was whipping the hair across both faces turned away from each other, both silent and waiting for the other to speak. Christine spoke first.

"I can't be with you tonight."

"Why?"

"I've met someone. Do you hate me?"

There was a long pause before Kit said, "No."

He looked at her, she looked at him.

"You should have told me before I came here. You should have told me on the phone."

"I wanted you to meet him. I think you'll both get along really well. I'm sure you'll like him."

He couldn't look at her. The injustice was bad enough, but the ignorance immeasurably worse. Sounds of honking, howls and laughter wafted to the balcony from the streets 20 odd floors below. He poured a shot of Jack Daniels. He studied it and ignored the noise. He would not get angry. Grin and bear it. He was hoping she would say something, get angry, anything.

"I hope you'll forgive me. Do you forgive me?" asked Christine.

He only wanted one thing. He wanted to make her pay. He wanted to crush her ribs, to pull her apart until she snapped. Of course, it will never happen. And now she's going, without paying, without thinking.

He heard himself saying, "There's nothing to forgive. What did I tell you before? If someone loves you, and I do still love you, forgiveness is part of the package. You don't have to say sorry to me."

"I know, no sorry, no thank you, I remember."

"Right, no 'sorry,' no 'thank you,' and especially no 'take care'."

They both smiled as he said this. They felt a bond between them which deepened their mutual sadness.

"But we have said sorry to each other many times," she said, smiling, her eyes mischievous, challenging.

"That's because we like to argue, and there were so few people worth arguing with."

"I remember," she said, "don't argue with people not worth arguing with."

"We are equals, that's why we fought all the time; it was a balanced fight though you won most of the close ones."

"All of the close ones," she said.

"That's right, all of the close ones, the 50/50 ones."

He remembered a time when he had been obsessed with her, when all he wanted to do was touch her. He felt ill at the thought of the hands touching someone else.

"You know, if you had taken care of me better, I never would have found someone else."

"Uh-huh," he said, thinking of a line in a song - "And now you make me feel ashamed because I've only got two hands." What made it so incongruous was the next line – "But I'm still fond of you.' He'd always been struck by the word 'fond,' it was so English, so polite.

"That's all you can say?" asked Christine, who was getting impatient, fed up; she could explode soon.

"Yeah, uh-huh. What the fuck do you know about the Smiths, anyway?"

That stung. "What the hell does a fucking band have to do with taking me for granted?"

"Nothing at all, absolutely nothing at all."

Her hand was trembling, holding a menthol cigarette.

"Who is paying for the next bottle?" asked Kelvin, flushed and grinning from the last bottle, and the rounds before that. Two of the present company, stirred out of listening to the murmuring sea, said, "I am."

"White, red or rosé?" asked Kelvin, and before the rest could gather themselves to answer, added, "Californian, Portuguese, Italian, French or Australian?"

"Since you're so hyper about everything and you are the designated group bartender, why don't you decide?" replied Amir.

"Tanqueray," pleaded Guru, who was ignored but not told to shut up.

Sunny had a bright idea. "Saké got or not?"

"Fuck you lah, saké. People drinking wine, you want saké," said Kelvin.

"Saké Japanese wine what," countered Sunny.

"Saké is saké. When we talk wine, we're talking about Burgundy, Beaujolais, shit like that, understand you dumb Cina apek bodoh," said Kelvin who was Chinese himself, so he could say such things.

"Yeah, kick his ass, Kelvin, go ahead, the fucker whole life talk cock only."

"Aahh, ooh, ahh, oi, owww, eh, pain lah fucker!"

The company around the table talked of being born in Portsmouth, of fathers from Scotland and the south-west coast of India, of mothers with Arabic, Turkish, Persian, Portuguese, Dutch and English blood, of being brought up in Johor Baru, Malacca, London and Singapore and they wondered which part of China Christine came from with a surname like 'Yeang.' No one knew; another day, another infuriating question, no matter, yam seng. They talked of the past, of people once known, of events and moments once happened, of fights all but forgotten. So easy to smile at and disregard now, but which once were important points of honour or pride, to be upheld at all cost. Stripes and fangs presented, now only fading, toothless and silly.

Between the shades of deep blue and indigo and the finality of black, stars could be seen in the heavens, unable, however, to shed any light on the vaguely excitable proceedings below. This was effected by strings of tiny light-bulbs arching around the beachfront terrace. On the tables, candles in large brown-tinted, black-stained glass goblets did their best to illuminate the faces bent over menus, deliberating over fish or steak, steamed, grilled or well-done.

"Remember your heart, dear," said the lady to her husband, concern etched on her face.

"Fuck the heart," he replied, "I'll have red meat on New Year's Eve if it kills me."

"My sister just had her second ..." "Which one? Jackie? Oh, so you're an uncle." "In addition to being a bastard."

"Notice how so few couples bother to look at each other, much less talk on this night of all nights," said Mike.

"Is that sad or pathetic?" asked Kamal.

"Perhaps they've run out of things to say," said Douglas.

"They look like they wished they were someplace else, with someone else," said Kamal.

"Frightening thought, to be stuck with someone simply out of habit," said Amir.

"The worst part is the realisation, and the acceptance," said David.

"Let's none of us get married. Amir's right. I don't want to keep up appearances. I want to be able to walk away if I have to," said Kelvin.

"Even if you find the right girl, the perfect woman?" asked Mike.

"The more perfect she is, the more painful it is," said Amir.

"It's tragic that people have to get married to find out slowly what they had guessed," said Douglas.

"It's better surely than being old alone, dying alone," said Kamal.

"Yeah, but one or the other will be left to mourn," said Kelvin.

"But they'll have children, family."

"How many children you know will put up with their parents when they're old?" asked Amir.

"Not many," replied the present company.

"Damn right, not many," said Amir.

In the delightful fervour of spinning tales, true, oft-repeated and in many cases quite ordinary and mundane, though, because of distance and time, taking on ever more mythic proportions, still the last sentence must come and the laughter must subside, and in that silence which grows more uncomfortable by the second, that confounding silence, the present company grows older, sadder, wiser in recognising a moment of knowledge, bitter and dissonant.

The cigarette smoke was exhaled loudly, expelled rather than released. She made up her mind and spoke, "Why don't you come with me to Georgetown tonight? We'll celebrate New Year together."

"Together with him? The three of us together, that would be perfect for you, wouldn't it?"

"No, not perfect, just o.k."

"You should have told me."

"You said that already."

"Yeah, I'm saying it again."

"If you're gonna yell at me, I'd better go."

"I'm not yelling!"

"You are … you were."

"O.k., I'm not anymore."

"Tomorrow he's all yours, and good luck to you both. But tonight, Chris, tonight, please, just for New Year's Eve …"

Mike said, "Do you guys remember that night Robert put tequila on the prawns?"

"Yeah, why did he do that?" asked Kamal.

"He was in good form, that's why," ventured Amir.

"That was a New Year's Eve, right?"

"At Kelvin's house," said Sunny.

"That's right," replied Douglas, "that was when Kamal puked and sat beside the drain the whole night."

"And Jessie," shouted Seng, "sat next to him for hours trying to pick him up."

Guru, grinning, added, "I wonder whether you were a good conversationalist that night, Kamal, I mean, what was it that attracted her to you that night beside the drain."

"I think what it was," chimed in Douglas, "was, you know, like in those National Geographic specials."

"Huh?"

"I don't know why I remember it, but anyway, there's this row of lobsters marching on the seabed and this fish appears …"

"Where're they going?"

"Huh? They're migrating, lah, going south or somewhere warm."

"Anyway, fuck lah, let me finish, can or not? This fish has a fucking small mouth and you wonder how on earth, I mean there's no way ..."

"What does the fish look like?" asked Sunny.

"It looks like your mother," said Kelvin.

"Fuck you, man, what's your problem?"

"Actually, it looks like a bawal, you know, flat, silver," continued Douglas, "and when it sees a lobster that has strayed, first thing, it breaks the antenna off, then this thing with heavy armour full of claws is helpless. Then it just, one by one, sucks all the legs of the lobster out and then the lobster can't move, and within seconds, seconds, man, nothing left, just the shell, full of holes."

"Who were we talking about?" asked David.

"Kamal, who got separated from the pack and was attacked by Jessie," replied Guru.

"She wasn't there that long, what, only a few minutes," said Kamal defensively.

"Are you kidding? I thought you both had fallen asleep in a squatting position," suggested Kelvin.

"Some people are capable of any horror," said Amir.

"You guys, you're so unfair. She wasn't trying to screw him, she was trying to be nice. You're so awful," appealed Yvonne.

"Gentlemen, you're being too cynical. Yvonne's right," said David. "I read this definition somewhere, this definition of love; if you and your beloved ..."

"Your what?" asked Kelvin.

"Your girlfriend. If you and your girlfriend are on a boat and the sea is choppy ..."

"Sea is what?"

"... big waves, and you're both seasick and you forget your discomfort simply because of the incredible joy you get from holding your loved one's head in your lap, when she is at her worst ..."

"When she has vomit all over her face ..."

"... then you know you're in love."

"Who said that?"

"Samuel Butler."

"You see," screamed Guru "you see what happens when you drink Tanqueray."

"Yes, your recall of English literature improves," replied Kelvin.

Again that uncomfortable, paralysing silence. Most of the diners had returned to their rooms for private celebrations or had disappeared to parties and bars. The tables were cleared and cleaned. A group of waiters leaned against the bar, relaxed and unbothered. A waiter strolled past with the good feeling in him that comes with the end of his shift, his last shift of the year. There was neither practical nor glorious ambition, only comfort in one's own circle, plans in one's head, but try as they might, the silence irritated, a dull gnawing feeling still persisted and no amount of happiness or goodwill could prevent it from surfacing. Yet more loss of time, without concrete result, without reward; it was tiresome, intangible. What was a proper life anyway? How was one to know if one was happy? Of all the idiocy. And to think that some people bothered. And to think that others listened.

The cause for the stagnancy which seemed to dog and paralyse proceedings was the fact that they felt safe together. Many a brave wanderer would gladly give up his kingdom and all he has built and created for the reassurance of a familiar face, presence; laugh. Differences of opinion were settled without resorting to playing on one's insecurities, preying on one's weaknesses, which often forces the other to react by being defensive or worse, irrational and immature, which meant the argument never ended, was merely postponed and remembered, stored away for later use.

Among the present company, all competition was settled in secondary school. Being friends for so long meant that no matter how badly you behave, your worth in your friend's eyes will not be altered significantly. They have seen you at your worst, and thus cannot be shocked. It takes a monumental effort, quite beyond the pale; to piss them off or impress them. They do not make you feel guilty and cannot make you feel worthless. Love was made for desertion; friendship was a happy accident to begin with. Unfortunately, with the passage of time, the circle of magic and spontaneity, of hilarity and amazement, once boundless and beyond a far horizon, irretrievably shrinks, despite all our best efforts, to within almost touching distance.

Fifteen minutes to the end of the year.

"I have to go," she said. "Tell Yvonne and the guys 'bye for me."

He looked at her eyes until she couldn't bear it and looked away. He was remembering a day eight years ago when a shop attendant told him, "You're looking very happy today, sir," and he had been surprised by that remark, taken aback by the incongruity of that smiling suggestion, for he had just heard the admission of a girl that she was seeing someone else. It was the Christmas/ New Year holidays and he had flown to London to see her. He had spent the better part of a beautiful, brisk winter's day with her in Camden Market shopping for presents for her relatives and her friends. He hadn't realized she was his for just a day, that she wasn't his at all.

The thought made him sick, bile crawled up his throat. He controlled it, swallowing, heaving short rapid breaths, eyes watering. He didn't want Christine to think he was crying. Concentrate, he was thinking, concentrate on the soundless images on the T.V. Never cry in front of a lady, they murder you for it later, in spite of themselves.

She was still waiting for his answer. Just one word and she could go. The fact that he wasn't taking this at all well meant she was almost home. She knew better than to say, "Are you all right?"

Yes, he was thinking, that was New Year's Eve too; in bloody London, and the pubs close at 11.15. Imagine not having the chance to kill yourself after 11.15. With her relatives and that girl in a tiny living room with a stifling heater. "Do me a favour, just pretend, they don't know yet." The women in that room were beautiful, the men old. Not a cigarette was in sight, not a hair out of place, drinking sherry (he would've given his soul for a double anything, fortunately, none was forthcoming), exceedingly polite, excruciatingly pedantic; and complimenting them for being a fine couple, and would he like another glass of sherry. "Not too many now," said Auntie, "have to wake up in the morning, ha ha."

Christine couldn't wait any longer. "I'll call you."

"Don't bother."

He listened to her footsteps escaping.

"How much time do we have? Fuck, chibai, only 10 more minutes," said Kelvin. "Oi, FUCKERS, 10 to 12 man, almost New Year, wake up, wake up, let's go."

Douglas sprang up and overturned a glass which flew and splashed onto David who woke up and fell backwards in the same instant, chair and all, which made Kamal laugh, which became hiccups, which prompted Yvonne to slap his back hard and repeatedly, bleating in her charming Cantonese accent, "Drink fast some more lah; yam seng some more lah."

"Yvonne," Kelvin interrupted, "don't whack him so hard lah, pity the bugger, he fucking can't breathe. David still lying on the ground, ah? Fucker pengsan or what? Get him up man. Don't leave him lying here, recycle everything."

Sunny was patting his pockets, muttering; "Fuck man, I lost my keys. Hey guys, I lost my keys. Did anybody see my keys?"

"We paid the bill ah? Paid already, right?" asked Kelvin.

Amir remembered. "Hey, we should go get Kit, lah, somebody should go get Kit. Who's gonna go and look for them?"

"O.K., so now, where we going?" inquired Kamal.

"To the water!" shouted Kelvin.

"To the beach," shouted Douglas and David.

Mike had a question. "We're going to the water, right, not on the water?"

"No, in the water," affirmed Kelvin, emphasizing 'in' by stamping his foot.

"In the water?"

"In the water."

"In the sea."

They walked in a ragged swaying formation.

The ritualistic, inevitable chant had started: "10, 9, 8 ..."

The balconies were full with young people, confident, brave, noisy.

"7, 6, 5 ..."

There was a crawl of cars in the streets. Marauding gangs of kids were massing, howling and hooting with the cars, banging on the cars. Some passengers were lying on the bonnets looking at the embracing sky speckled and pierced with pinholes of light that shone from the past, pure and ancient. The moon caught and burned the edges of a silent procession of clouds. The police were nowhere to be seen.

"4, 3, 2 ..."

Revelers were jumping into the pool, jostling, shoving and shrieking, wearing shiny paper hats and masks, blowing paper flutes which uncurled rapidly into faces, tapping gently and retreating.

"1!"

Feroz Dawson Biography.

••••

Feroz Dawson was born in 1966. His parents, Leslie Dawson and Faridah Merican, divorced soon after he was born. He grew up with his mother in Petaling Jaya. He was involved in theatre by the age of six and by the time he was 10, he had appeared in four plays. While other boys were doing homework, he was attending rehearsals. "I was always surrounded by adults, listening to what they said – "Theatre people never stopped talking" – and developed an ear, so useful later as a writer, for the way people spoke.

He went to the United States as a Journalism student, but changed his major, after the first semester, to Film. When he returned from the US, Feroz worked in a production house shooting commercials for TV, starting as crew member, eventually becoming an assistant director. Feroz directed two music videos that were nominated for seven awards in the first music video awards in Malaysia in 1996. These videos led him to directing commercials in Indonesia.

Feroz wrote short stories after work. He did it for a variety of reasons, the main one being Akira Kurosawa who said that if you wanted to be a film director, you had to be a writer.